OF NIGHT AND LIGHT

By

Caroline Coxon

with artwork by

Daria Kudla

Published by New Generation Publishing in 2014

Copyright © Caroline Coxon 2014

First Edition

The author asserts the moral right under the Copyright, Designs and Patents Act 1988 to be identified as the author of this work.

All Rights reserved. No part of this publication may be reproduced, stored in a retrieval system or transmitted, in any form or by any means without the prior consent of the author, nor be otherwise circulated in any form of binding or cover other than that which it is published and without a similar condition being imposed on the subsequent purchaser.

www.newgeneration-publishing.com

New Generation **Publishing**

After many years as a teacher for children with special needs, Caroline Coxon became a full-time writer in 2002. By day she's a copywriter, but in the wee small hours of the night when no-one's watching she writes screenplays, poems and stories.

Chapter 1

Here I am slathering gel in my hair in a desperate attempt to make it stand up spiky and outside it's slashing down with rain, like every other mind-suckingly miserable day since we left London, but I don't want to sound negative.

Alice is singing in the garden in her nightie. To say she's singing is not strictly accurate. I mean, *she* thinks she's singing but the rest of the world thinks a cat's being mangled in the lawn-mower.

The noise is really doing my head in and I shout out to her, "Shut up, will you, fruitcake?" But of course she doesn't, so I slam the window and the mirror above the wash-basin cracks. Right down the middle like a jagged streak of lightning. Shit! How could that have happened? It's a bit of a shock really. And now, when I look in the mirror, my face is cut in half, which I wouldn't mind because I only like one half of my face anyway.

Then I think about Alice, out there in the pouring rain in only her nightie and I suppose someone should do something, preferably not me, so I call out to Mum, "Alice is in the garden."

Mum says in a wheedly voice, "Couldn't you just get her in, Rosa?" and when I don't answer for about a millisecond she shouts, "NOW!"

That'll teach me to open my big mouth.

I stomp down the stairs loudly to Make A Point and go out into the garden. It's still slashing down with rain. Alice is in the middle of the lawn and she could be in one of those wet T-shirt contests only it's a nightie and her chest is completely flat. She has her face turned to the sky and she's spinning round and round with her arms outstretched. (I did tell you she was mad).

"Alice," I call out, but she doesn't notice and my mascara starts running down my face like I've been crying. Then I grab her by the shoulder and she smiles sweetly at me and says, "It's raining, Rosa."

"Really? I hadn't noticed..."

I don't know why I wasted my breath. Sarcasm is lost on Alice, like most other things.

So I drag her towards the house. And all the while she's looking over her shoulder and then she squeaks, "Hare!" Hare like a rabbit, I mean. I worked that out later but, at the time, I think she's saying "Hair!" like the stuff that sprouts from your head and other places, so I say, "Yeah, well now mine'll go all flat. Thanks a bunch, Alice."

And I pull her though the door into the kitchen and we're dripping like unfortunate wet knickers, and I'm so livid the water droplets have turned to steam.

I get a massive amount of sympathy from Mum when I look in drawers and cupboards and everywhere for a hair-dryer. She's far too busy taking care of Alice, which makes a change.

"Where is it?" I say (more of a screech, I suppose) and she says, "Your sense of humour? I think you left it in Notting Hill, didn't you?"

Well, *she's* not the one who's soaked to the unmentionable regions and about to catch double pneumonia. "The hair-dryer!" I shout, and she says, so calmly I want to slap her, "We have towels."

And all the while, Alice is muttering under her breath about rain-dark snails. (Oh, I forgot to mention that she spouts weird poetry). And she gets to a bit where she says, not under her breath, "While we wait in the dark room..." and there's an almighty crack and I just catch her smiling before the power cuts out.

Chapter 2

Living down here in Somerset is like being in The Dark Ages, especially when there's a power cut. This is a joke that isn't even funny.

Well, *I* think it's like being in The Dark Ages and I know Dad thinks so too because straight after the crack there's a roar from upstairs and some interesting swearing and the sound of furniture being dragged across the floor.

I suppose it wasn't his fault he lost his job and we ended up here, but you'd think he'd be a bit more apologetic instead of raging about the place like a bull with a bee-sting on his bottom.

He used to be a graphic designer.

I expect he still is a graphic designer, only you wouldn't know it.

What gets me is when Mum just pretends nothing's happening as though that'll cancel out the things that *are* happening. With all the crashing and banging, which is impossible to ignore, all she does is she bows her head and carries on stirring some sort of cake mix with a wooden spoon. And she hums.

And Alice goes white as skimmed milk and glides across to the window where she rubs a hole in the condensation with her finger and it makes that squeaky sound that could drive you insane. (Too late for Alice). Then she peers through it into the garden like it's a telescope.

I have to escape somewhere and there's only my room, well, my *half* of the room because the other bit is filled up with all Alice's airy-fairy stuff.

Mum and Dad's bedroom door is open and, if it wasn't so typical of this hovel we live in, I could have wet myself laughing. I'm already soaking anyway so it wouldn't have made much difference.

There is Dad still in his pyjamas even though it's the middle of the afternoon. He's ranting and raving with water pouring through the ceiling onto his computer and the bed's all pushed to one side and he's shouting, "Sally, Sal, the master switch, for Christ's sake flick the effing master switch."

Parents can be very undignified sometimes.

And I can just see Mum rolling her eyes and wishing that Dad had some sort of master switch so you could turn *him* off when he gets moody.

Not that I'm sticking up for her at all. She used to be quite sensible when we had a life, but since we moved she's turned into some sort of New Age Tree-Hugger. I'm pretty relieved that none of my friends can see her. They'd probably think she was a bag lady.

So I creep by Dad's bedroom before he notices me and go into my (half) bedroom and shut the door.

The mirror's still cracked, surprise, surprise, and I look disgusting. All my make-up's running down my face in black and flesh-coloured rivulets and any crazy person who bothered to give me a second glance would see my birthmark, which I don't want to talk about.

Suddenly it goes all bright in this gloomy hole of a room and I think the power must be back but it's just the sun coming out after the rain.

I'm not a great fan of fresh air but for once I open the window and gaze out at the garden which doesn't look at all bad - all sparkly with raindrops and freshly washed like one of those shampoo adverts, and birds singing.

But then they stop.

And then it gets weird and just a bit scary, though I'd be the last person to admit it because that's not exactly cool.

In the middle of the lawn is a huge skanky rabbit-thing which is actually a hare and when I say huge I'm not exaggerating.

Then Alice comes trotting out of the back door one hand stretched out towards this creature, which is staring goggle-eyed at her. She's crying out, "I'm coming, I'm coming out of the door we never opened..."or some such utter drivel.

And that's when a solid block of greyness plummets out of Dad's bedroom window and misses Alice by about a centimetre and shatters into a thousand pieces on the garden path. Goodbye, computer monitor, and so very nearly my sister, whose face is paralysed into a silent scream. And I don't blame her.

As I rush down stairs I hear Dad shouting, "It's broken I tell you. It's bloody well broken." And Mum saying calmly in her calm voice that means she's not calm, "Well, if it wasn't before I'm sure it is..."

Then she must have looked out of the window because the next thing she says, except it's not saying but screaming, is, "Oh dear God, Alice!"

I sprint into the garden and I can hear a baby crying and then it's not a baby after all but Alice. A strange wailing sound comes out of her mouth and her whole body is shaking.

Mum arrives just behind me and flings her arms round Alice and says, "Silly Daddy!"

I think my mouth might have dropped open. "Silly Daddy? Silly Daddy?" I squawk. "He could have killed her!"

And he could have. He almost did.

But Mum flashes me A Warning Look and says, "No harm done. Come on Alice. Come inside and I'll make you a nice cup of hot chocolate."

I say, "Oh, for God's sake!" even though I am seriously speechless. What is it about mums that make them think a cup of hot chocolate could possibly do anything to make a life-threatening situation somehow…not?

They disappear inside and I'm so mad I kick out with my Doc Martens and as all the glass splinters fly through the air I notice there are moving pictures in each one like cartoons of people running.

But maybe it's a trick of the light.

Chapter 3

Making a scene is not very much fun when no-one's watching.

I storm up to my half-room again. My head's like a tumble-dryer spinning round with random thoughts about phoning Childline or escaping from an uncertain fate before it's too late and I die a horrible death at the hands of my lunatic father, crushed by a carelessly lobbed piece of computer hardware.

I finish fixing my face and I'm wishing I had someone sane to talk to and then I think of Jules back in Notting Hill. She's nearly sane. But there's no mobile phone signal here unless you hang most of the way out of the window sideways.

That makes me think of how it was before. Before my fourteenth birthday. Before NOW. Before the Dark Times. It's hard to imagine that once I thought life in Notting Hill was so woefully dull.

I'd give about three year's clothes allowance, if I still had a clothes allowance, to be back there, with Dad slouching off to work in deepest darkest Soho in a foul temper. (Much cheaper than going on the train). And Mum pretending to be busy raising money for some charity to do with poor people with important committee meetings in wine bars at lunchtime. The charity ladies, that is, not the poor people. I expect they're busy raising money for us now, sniggering to themselves and knitting us woolly socks made out of recycled sheep, ready for the winter.

And Alice in her special private school for special private children which suited me fine because she's a total embarrassment and it meant I could hang out with Jules and not have Alice trailing along, eyes all shiny with sisterly adoration.

Good old Jules. I know I'd feel better if I could bleat to her so maybe I'll see if the phone works in the kitchen instead.

It's as though Earlier hadn't happened.

Smoke pours out of the sides of the oven and Mum is poking boiling potatoes with a knife to see if they're dead yet (her cooking is that bad).

Alice is drawing some sort of perfectly symmetrical elaborate squiggle at the table. Sometimes she's not even looking at what she's doing and still the crayon whizzes round the paper as though it has a mind of its own. She can be very clever for someone who's mad.

And me? Well, I'm holding my phone above my head at all different angles still trying to get a signal.

"It's the valley," says Mum, not even looking up and I say, "It's the pits," and throw the phone on to the table. It makes Alice jump but not as much as the computer monitor did.

On the draining board there's a pile of strange gnarled objects covered in earth. "What are those?" I ask, and Mum tells me they're carrots that she grew herself.

"Carrots? I thought carrots were orange and... well, carrot-shaped."

"And come wrapped in plastic from the supermarket?" snaps Mum, so I know I've Touched A Nerve, which I must remember for future use. But surely she's not expecting me to eat those things?

And then she opens the oven door with a flourish and pulls out the cremated remains of what might be a cake with a triumphant expression on her face so it's hard to say anything very harsh after that. I'm not entirely cruel to the elderly.

Through the ceiling we can hear Dad stomping about and shouting things at inanimate objects as though they will be able to understand. This is called a

Pathetic Fallacy which you can look up if you don't believe me, and I think it's pretty pathetic, personally.

And Alice looks up at the ceiling and says, "I think Daddy must love his bedroom very much."

"Why do you say that, darling?" Mum asks. And Alice answers, "Because he hardly ever comes out of it, does he?"

Mum and I are just smiling at each other which is unusual and quite nice when we hear Dad thundering down the stairs as though he's heard what Alice said, but he couldn't have.

He sticks his head round the door and says, "Ah, the heady aroma of one of Mum's special cakes." Then he comes in and sits down all smiles next to Alice.

At least he's wearing a dressing-gown.

Chapter 4

At supper we pretend to be A Normal Family and it works quite well for a while. The lights pretend to be normal lights too but that works less well because they can't stop flickering madly.

When I say normal, I have to admit that I don't really know what normal is. For instance, is it normal that Alice's head suddenly snaps round towards the window and she mutters about creatures panting through the undergrowth, hearts beating wildly?

No, I didn't think so.

Mum swishes the curtains closed, saying, "Just a fox, I expect." She glances at me in a surreptitious kind of way as though hoping I hadn't noticed that she doesn't quite believe it either. And Dad begins to sing "The fox went out on a chilly night," and Alice gurgles like a blocked plughole. And me? I resign myself to the fact that someone's probably going mad and I hope it isn't me.

Then Alice's eyes start to roll and a voice that doesn't seem to come from her at all whispers, "Something else is alive in dark night's forest and..." But Mum interrupts, just when it was getting interesting.

"Well, I think it's time for bed, don't you?"

I didn't think it was time for bed, actually. Particularly not at the same time as my kid sister, but Mum has to keep on just like mums do. It must be in the job description, I suppose. "First day at your new school tomorrow! Isn't it exciting?"

Exciting? Exciting is not the first word that comes into my head and my hand shoots to the bad side of my face and I hate it for doing that without permission. And Mum adds, "Then just a few days until the holidays."

I still don't see why we can't just start next term and I must have said it out loud because Mum says, "And spend the summer knowing no-one?"

That would suit me just fine.

So there I am tossing and turning in my lumpy uncomfortable bed and wishing the curtains were a whole lot thicker because they're all flappy in the breeze and the moon keeps shining on my face, as though I need moonlight to show me how ugly it is.

And Alice, of course, is sleeping like a baby. That's what the expression is, but I don't think it's very good because all the babies I've ever known do things in their nappies when they're asleep. Alice may be mad but she's not incontinent.

I must have dropped off to sleep for a bit because I remember having the strangest sort of dream which I won't bore you with because I can't bear it when people tell me their dreams. It was set in medieval times and there was a young couple all loved-up skipping through the woods and they come across a baby and the girl wants it for herself because it's so pretty but the boy's not keen...but she picks it up anyway and, that huge hare appears from nowhere and suddenly... There, I told you it was boring hearing other people's dreams. Yawn.

Then I wake up and Alice has gone.

Chapter 5

I'm used to Alice wandering, in fact it's become quite a pain lately. I've got better things to do with my nights than chase around after her, like try to get some sleep for instance.

At first I put my pillow over my head and try to ignore the fact that her bed's empty. She's probably just gone to the loo or something. That's what I tell myself, but I'm not very convincing. It doesn't take long for me to realise that there's no way I'll get to sleep until I know where she is, so I drag my weary body out from under the blankets. As I do, there's a kind of murmuring coming through the window, which is open behind the flappy curtains.

Apart from being annoying, moonlight has its advantages, one being that I can see right across the garden. In the far corner there's a yew tree – well, that's what Mum told me, though I wouldn't know, to be honest. Under it, huddled together are Mum and Someone Else who looks like an old lady but it's too far away to be absolutely sure and they both have their backs to me. That's where the murmuring's coming from.

Gliding towards them across the lawn, looking like a ghostly angel in her long white nightie, is Alice. I think she's probably sleep-walking. I'm just about to call out to her when, out of nowhere, an enormous owl swoops down at her head with a screech like a thousand simultaneous finger nails on a blackboard. I duck stupidly as though it's me being dive-bombed and Alice crumples to the ground in a heap.

Mum races over to her. The old lady, if it was an old lady, disappears. Into thin air. And that's another stupid expression because whoever heard of air that was thick?

I grab my dressing gown and stumble down the stairs and I'm only halfway across the kitchen when I meet Mum and Alice, who looks perfectly okay considering she's just been attacked by a vicious bird.

"Alice was sleepwalking," Mum says unnecessarily. Duh! "Would you take her back to bed?" So I do. I'm too tired to bother asking what Mum was doing in the garden and who was the old lady person? I tell myself I'll ask in the morning...but somehow I never get round to it. I'm good at that.

Flat on her back in bed now, hands clasped on her chest, Alice looks like one of those stone effigies on a grave. I keep asking her and asking her what really happened and she keeps saying, "I can't remember, Rosa."

I could throttle her.

I nearly *do* throttle her when she begins to drift off to sleep again. Under her breath she's mumbling something about being half in love with easeful death. I go "Aaaaargh!" and stick my head under the pillow again. By the time I've said, "I do wish you'd stop that, Alice," she's asleep. And I'm wide awake.

Thanks for nothing, Alice.

And those curtains are *still* flapping so I crawl out of bed *again* to close the window. As I do, I see the old woman on the lawn looking up at the cottage. Except, perhaps it's me who's going mad because I blink and it isn't an old woman at all but that hare, which does a kind of back flip and dives into the bushes.

Mum always says that eating cheese give you strange dreams and I must have wolfed down about six pounds of Cheddar without noticing because the medieval people are at it again in my mind. The baby has turned hideous and squirmy so they put it down on the ground by a pond. And the girl looks at her reflection in the water and a horrible blemish spreads like a stain across her face just like my birthmark. And she turns round and the boy has gone. But the baby hasn't.

Remind me never to eat cheese ever again.

Chapter 6

And another thing. Who needs an alarm clock when they've got an annoying mother like mine?

"Rise and shine, sweethearts!"

Grrrrr. I hate morning people.

If I'd had an alarm clock I'd have buried it in the garden anyway because today's going to be the worst day of the rest of my life. Starting the new school. Yippee doo.

"The sun has got his hat on! Hip hip hip hooray!" wafts up the stairs all out of tune.

Shut *up*, mother!

School is too good a name for where I'm being sent. And the school thinks so too because it calls itself a Rural Community College. We'll probably be taught muck-spreading and how dig stones out of horses' hooves etc.

"Breakfast's on the table, girls." Will she never give up sounding cheerful, my mum?

She *knows* it takes me ages to get ready with the camouflage make-up. That's not camouflage like soldiers use, by the way, though I have considered it, ha ha, but then I'd have to spend the day hiding in the bushes. (Come to think of it, that sounds like a good idea). No, my make-up is meant to be flesh-coloured only it's a bit too orangey for my liking, but slightly better than the violent purply-red of my birthmark.

Then there's the school uniform. It needs a lot of attention to make it halfway presentable. I roll the hideously ordinary navy blue skirt up at the waist and knot the tie so it's only about six inches long and you can't see the crest. Thick black tights, designer-distressed with blunt scissors, purple Doc Martens and I'm nearly satisfied.

Of course, just when I'm about to go downstairs ready to refuse breakfast Mum shouts, "Does anyone have any idea what time it is?" which is her pathetic grown-up way of trying to be sarcastic.

That sets Alice off reciting, "Defer no time, delays have dangerous ends," which I know is a bit of Shakespeare and I'm sure she hasn't ever read any.

A little pain the shape of a needle stab-stab-stabs inside my head.

Then for some reason I start retching into the wash basin.

I'm positive I'm not anxious about today, just seriously hacked off. Maybe it's food poisoning? That wouldn't be a surprise with Mum's cooking.

And Mum carries on in sarcastic mode, yelling, "That was a rhetorical question, Rosa. Not requiring an answer, only for you to get your backside down the stairs. NOW!" She doesn't mention Alice, of course, who is still upstairs as well.

There's nothing more annoying than being told to do something you were on the point of doing anyway, even if you didn't want to.

It's quite therapeutic clumping my boots all the way down the stairs behind Alice. You should try it.

You wouldn't believe what Alice looks like. She could have been in one of those Enid Blyton books Mum raves on about as though they're Good Literature. She wears white ankle socks and sandals and her hair is in plaits, tied up with ribbons. Worse still, her skirt reaches at least two inches below her knee. I would positively *die* if I looked like that and I can't help thinking that she might too, with the teasing, but probably it's what people at Rural Community Colleges wear all the time.

Mum is busy rummaging through drawers muttering, "I know it's here somewhere," then she fishes out a wrinkled black and white photo and waves it under our noses. "There you go, I found it!" she says. Yes, I can see that, mother.

In the photo are two girls who look weirdly like me and Alice only they're not. They're in old-fashioned school uniform a bit like Alice is wearing today which must be why Mum wanted to show us. One of them is her, only younger, and the other makes me shiver a bit because it's my hardly-ever-mentioned-and-I-don't-know-why Auntie Deborah, who has a birthmark identical to mine and I used to think I was the only one ever.

"Who's that?" says Alice pointing at Auntie Deborah. I'm glad she does because I want Mum to tell me something about her but I wouldn't lower myself to appear interested. Mum goes a funny pink colour and says, "Don't you remember, Alice? That's your Auntie Deborah. My sister."

"You haven't got a sister," Alice giggles, and skips out of the room.

She's right about that because Auntie Deborah is dead.

Mum opens her mouth to speak but no words come out. I don't even bother to open my mouth and scoot out of the kitchen.

I think it's better than staying there in An Atmosphere Of Awkwardness.

Chapter 7

I don't know what to think about Mum and the Auntie Deborah thing so I don't think anything at all. I find it less tiring.

Instead, I chase after Alice and say, "What's keeping you? You're going to make me late again." It makes her smile, thank goodness. Alice likes being teased sometimes.

We grab our schoolbags and I say, "Let's hit the road, kid!" And then she can't possibly, possibly stop herself from quoting, "And I - I took the one less travelled by and that has made all the difference."

What would make all the difference would be if she would stop spouting pigging frigging poetry, which I tell her and she shrugs and says, "I don't mean to, it kind of comes out without me asking."

We just reach the garden gate when Mum appears on the doorstep and shouts, "Have fun! And Rosa, you will take care of your sister, won't you?"

It would have been nice if she had said, "You will take care of yourself, won't you?" But she didn't, so I mutter, "Yeah, thanks for the concern, Mummy," which is me being sarcastic in a not pathetic way.

Glancing back, I notice Dad waving at us out of the window but I don't wave back. He couldn't even be bothered to come downstairs to say goodbye. Goody-goody Alice waves though, and looks at me like I've murdered a fluffy kitten.

"Well, I wouldn't mind spending the day in my jim-jams doing sod all, like Dad," I say and Alice says she hasn't got any jim-jams. Which she hasn't. She only has floatie nighties. So that's the end of that conversation.

Our walk to school is indescribable but I'll try. In

Notting Hill it was pavements and dog poo and pedestrian crossings and being cool sauntering past Starbucks and Pizza Express with Jules. And me ignoring boys by pretending to window-shop and Jules not ignoring boys with lingering looks in their direction, which were always returned because she's the attractive one.

Here, it's trudging along a rutted muddy cart track, knee-deep in graspy grass beside some quite spookily dark woods. A bunch of trees, that's all they are, but somehow they give off the feeling that Their Eyes Are Upon Me. I conclude I must've been reading too many fantasy novels because trees don't stare at people in real life.

Once, I even think I see that old woman crouching in the undergrowth but I look again and it's a twisted root. Should have had some breakfast because my head's quite swimmy but I wouldn't give Mum the satisfaction.

When it's just me and Alice we can have quite sensible conversations occasionally.

"Are you worried about today?" I ask her and she answers, "Why should I be worried?"

I think, "You should be worried because you look like someone from the distant past and you're rather odd and I expect you're going to be bullied mercilessly." What comes out of my mouth is, "No reason, just wondering."

And she says, "No-one will notice your birthmark, Rosa." And I hate her and I love her at the same moment because that's the squirmy maggot eating me up inside.

She puts her arm round me and I'd like to put my arm round her too but something stops me and I stiffen up and shrug her off. She doesn't seem to mind. Alice can be very forgiving, or maybe it's that she's so soft in the head that she doesn't even notice when people are unkind. I haven't worked it out yet.

Whatever the case, at that precise moment, I'm really grateful.

Chapter 8

The school playground looks much like any school playground, by which I mean it could have been in Notting Hill or anywhere really. It isn't like a ploughed field or a peat bog or anything which is what I half expected of a Rural Community College.

The natives are not friendly but who gives a toss? Stuff them. Alice has disappeared somewhere and I'm standing on my own looking unconcerned and nonchalant. There's a gang of peasant girls staring at me like I'm from The Planet Zog which to them I probably am, because unlike them I have Style. Still, it's rude to whisper and point, isn't it? As if I care.

One of the girls has hair so ginger it's tangerine and I wonder if it came out of a bottle, though why anyone would actually choose hair that colour is a mystery. She has freckles too so unless she dabbed them on with a paintbrush, I'm guessing it's for real.

She must be the leader of the girlie gang because all the others cluster round her and, whenever she speaks, they laugh like silly sycophants. I had to look that last word up to check I had it right which is difficult when you can't spell it but you know what it means. Here you go: Servile self-seekers who attempt to win favour by flattering influential people. Exactly.

With her eyes on me to be absolutely sure I'm watching, she struts about like a cockerel, if that's what cockerels do, and puts on what she must think is a posh accent. It doesn't cover up her Somersetness which for some reason uses Zs instead of Ss like - Zomerzet. Uh?

"We have to walk like this actually on account of having pokers shoved up our bottoms," she says. How unutterably childish! And the sycophants shriek with laughter as though they've heard something funny or clever.

I'm so not impressed.

I give them the finger, though whether or not they can understand that insult is anyone's guess. Making my way towards the school building, shoulders back, head up, as if I *did* have a poker shoved up my bottom, to be honest, I can hear Ginger Nut saying, "Well, that wasn't great sport, was it girls?" And then there's a load of clucking noises and a glance shows me they're all flapping their arms like chickens. One thing I'm *not* is chicken but it's beneath my dignity even to acknowledge their existence so I carry on up the steps to the school.

As if that experience isn't enough to last three lifetimes, at the top of the steps is a boy. Boys are things to be avoided. He leans against the wall in a casual pose that's so casual it's obviously put on.

He grabs my arm and I try to fend him off without appearing to be bothered, which is tricky.

"Sorry about her," he says, taking me by surprise. Which is a surprise. The school entrance is my escape route but just before it, my curiosity gets the better of me and I find myself blurting out, "What have you got to be sorry about?"

I just catch the words, "Sorry that she's my sister," before I slam the door behind me and probably in his face too.

Rosa One, Rural Scum Nil.

Chapter 9

Somehow I manage to find Room 4B which is meant to be my classroom because it says so on a printout of my timetable. Printout? That's highly advanced and unexpected for this Neolithic Place of So-Called Learning.

The room is empty. Well, when I say empty there is no-one in it, but there are chairs and desks and a whiteboard and similar, just in case you were wondering. The window looks out onto the playground and I peer out of it like one of those police surveillance people who doesn't want to be seen.

In one corner are those silly tarts all huddled together probably plotting their next pathetic insulting little scheme designed to get the better of me, which it won't. Right in the centre is The Queen of Tarts whose name I'll abbreviate to GN because I'm so sick of writing Ginger Nut. She's not worth the effort.

In the other corner there is a whole crowd of mostly boys in a circle playing some sort of game like pinball pushing something from one side to another but I can't see the ball or whatever it is they're playing with.

I stop trying to see what it is anyway because on the other side of the school fence I notice the old woman. Maybe not *the* old woman but certainly *an* old woman.

Watching.

Me.

Or that's what it looks like.

Is she some sort of sicko?

Just lately my brain doesn't know what to think about anything what with being dragged from civilisation to the Dark Ages and so on but before it goes into meltdown (my brain not the Dark Ages) GN steams across the playground to the pinball game yelling something fit to bust seventy eardrums. Either that or she's opening her mouth very wide for no reason because I can't hear much through the window.

Then, with a creeping sort of sickness, I realise that the pinball isn't a ball at all.

It's Alice.

It's Alice they're pushing from one side of the circle to the other and now she's collapsed, sprawled out on the playground and GN is yelling again and the crowd backs away like she's a Rottweiler with rabies.

Now it's my turn to start steaming. I'm half way down the corridor crashing through double door after double door when Brother of GN appears sprinting towards me, shouting, "I think you might want to…"

I don't hear the rest of it because I'm already past him and through another double door which swings shut behind me and there's Alice crying, her knees all bloody, and GN half carrying her.

Alice sobs, "I couldn't see you, Rosa," and GN says, "There, sweetheart, I told you we'd find her."

And I say, "What the hell have you morons done to my sister?"

GN gives me An Icy Look and says, "You're welcome. Please don't mention it." Then she stomps off.

I suppose she expected me to be grateful.

In the meantime, GN's Brother has arrived on the scene and has seen everything. Everything. Without saying a word, but his grinning face says it all, he claws the air like a cat and makes a Mi…aowwwwww sound. Then he follows after GN, leaving me to pick up the pieces that were once my sister.

I wish Alice wasn't such an embarrassment.

I wish I didn't have to look after her.

I wish she didn't make me feel so guilty, just the sight of her.

I wish I was a million miles away from this dump and back in Notting Hill (although that's quite a bit closer).

Chapter 10

The rest of that first day at school is a bit of a blur. The school nurse cleans up Alice's knees and Alice says, yes she *would* like to stay at school, no she *wouldn't* like to go home early. Which is more than can be said for me.

I'd give anything to do just that. Except…go home? I don't even know where my home *is* anymore. The nearest I've got to a home is in Notting Hill and, as I said, that's a long way away even if I was exaggerating ever so slightly when I said a million miles.

And our lovely house is sold to Someone Else so it wouldn't do that much good if I turned up out of nowhere, barged in and took over my bedroom again, which I expect has been repainted because not many people like purple walls and black ceilings.

Arriving home that afternoon, or…arriving at The Hovel Where I Live At The Moment, is less of a blur and more of a waking-quaking nightmare.

Alice has not said a word the entire walk back, in a sort of trance, which I consider is probably shock. I'm not feeling much like talking to anyone anyway so it doesn't bother me that much.

I open the kitchen door and there is Mum. Her hair, which used to be so neat in a French plait, is loose and has leaves and twigs in it. My mouth drops open. It seems to do that quite a lot recently. (If you don't believe me look at the bit where Dad chucks the computer).

She starts off saying, "Did you have a good day at…"when Alice practically crawls in behind me, her knees oozing more blood.

Mum rushes over crying out, "Oh Alice, what have they done to you?" and that seems to snap Alice out of her dreamy state because her eyes blink a couple of times and then she says, "I think I'm going to enjoy it very much at my new school."

My mouth drops open again because I can't think of another description for what it does and Dad bounds in and booms, "I'm glad to hear it, honeybun!" and dances her round the kitchen and everyone's laughing and smiling.

Everyone but me.

Why do I bother?

Most of all, why do I bother to worry about my stupid sister?

Chapter 11

There's one thing I quite like about this place and that's the hammock slung between two apple trees in the garden. Well, you wouldn't expect apple trees in the house would you? (From that piece of outstandingly witty writing you can probably tell that I'm feeling better).

This hammock is deep and stripy and if you can ever manage to get yourself in it without tipping out of the other side you can be quite snuggled up and hidden from view except for the curvy bulge of your body which rather gives you away. It also helps if you don't suffer from sea-sickness.

Anyway, I'm rocking gently side to side, feeling quite drowsy in the evening sunshine and Dad appears in the garden dressed in his city suit. Mum's already out there cutting roses and other prickly things and she's wearing a moth-eaten straw hat all askew and a dress that looks like she made it from a pair of old flowery curtains. Groan.

"Ye Gods and Little Fishes, where *did* you get that dress?" says Dad. Hee hee.

"A charity shop. I thought I'd save the Versace for tea with the vicar," replies Mum. I can't help being a tiny bit impressed. Go Mum!

Dad isn't impressed. "There's no need to be..." he starts, but Mum's quick as a wink with her interruption.

"Sarcastic? The thing is Keith, I wasn't being sarcastic. I love being back here."

"You love being back here, do you?"

Didn't she just say that, Dad? Duh! What is it with grown-ups?

"Yes, I love being back here," she replies, just to make sure he really gets it.

"So all that Deborah stuff from the past was...?"

"I have to face it one day, Keith."

If I had antennae on top of my head, by now they'd have been quivering.

Dad grunts. Grunts can mean so many different things. I'm not sure what that one meant but perhaps Mum can translate.

"You losing your job was probably..." she falters.

I hold my breath. Dangerous ground that, mother. If I were you I'd change the subject. She must have heard me thinking.

"Are you off out?" she says, all cheery.

Dad's voice isn't all cheery. More sneery. "No, I thought I'd just hang around here and dig the garden wearing my best suit, newly back from the dry-cleaners."

"Now who's being..?" There's a meaningful pause.

(There are an awful lot of meaningful pauses when Mum and Dad have a conversation).

"Of course I'm off out, woman!"

Now there's a huge pause. A pregnant pause you might say if they weren't far too old to have a baby.

"Is it a secret? Where you're going?"

Now it starts to get even more interesting. I hold myself motionless in the hammock which is quite a feat, like lying still on a plate of jelly.

"No more of a secret than the mysterious things *you* get up to, Sally!"

Did he see out of the window that night too? The murmurings under the yew tree? The old woman?

"What are you talking about, Keith?" Yes, what's he talking about?

"I'm not blind you know, Sally. Why don't you invite her in?"

There's another humungous pause and I stick one ear out over the side of the canvas, determined not to miss the next bit.

Then the hammock tips too far and I fall out.

It should have been funny. No-one laughs.

Mum and Dad kind of harrumph.

It's as though That Conversation Has Never Taken Place.

Chapter 12

It's as though that conversation has never taken place until much later when dinner's on the table and there's no sign of Dad, and Mum's pretending not to mind when he comes bursting in through the door, his nose and cheeks all red so it's obvious he's been drinking. Obvious to me, at any rate, because I've seen it all before.

He bounds over to Mum and grabs her round the waist and whirls her round the kitchen which is further proof that Alcohol Has Passed His Lips, if further proof were needed. Alice giggles and I maintain a mature and disapproving silence.

"I think I've landed myself a job!" he burbles. "How about *that*, girls?"

Then he chortles. Chortles is one of those words that you find in old comics like The Beano but it seems to fit here. I like to be a bit adventurous in my use of vocabulary.

Mum doesn't. All she can manage to say is, "A job? How nice!"

Alice says, "Oh Daddy, now perhaps Mum can wash your pyjamas!" which nobody understands but me and then I chortle as well although I wish I could think of a different way of describing it. Also I wish I hadn't chortled because it makes me look as though I am enjoying myself.

"So," says Mum portentously, which is a very impressive word, "Aren't you going to tell us about this new job, then?"

Dad begins to tell us but he isn't able to get very far at all. He says, "Well, I went up to The Manor House…" and Mum yells, "You did what?"

Dad looks crestfallen and I have to feel a little bit

sorry for him. He says, "I told you I..."and Mum leaps in again about an inch from his nose screeching, "You went cap in hand to Lord and Lady Muck and asked them for a job?"

"It wasn't like that," says Dad. "Tris and I..."

Mum interrupts again. (I do wish she'd let people finish their sentences).

"Tris, now is it? The very person that wants to destroy..." then she stops before the end of her own sentence which is even more annoying because I want to know what she's talking about (for a change).

"Destroy? Destroy what?" asks Dad. Well done him. Saves me asking. It doesn't work though because all Mum says is, "It doesn't matter."

And runs out of the kitchen.

Oh, we did have such a jolly family meal after that.

As you can imagine.

Chapter 13

Next morning I make my way down the stairs ridiculously early, at least three minutes before it's time to set off to school and I'm fully expecting An Atmosphere.

To my dismay, instead of An Atmosphere, which can be fun to watch, sitting in the kitchen with Mum as if she owns the place is The Old Woman. Has Mum taken leave of her senses? I won't say my mouth dropped open again because that's getting repetitive (but it did).

"Rosa!" announces Mum, "This is Megan, an old friend of the family."

So... being an old friend of the family gives someone permission to follow us about and spy on our every move does it? I don't actually say that out loud but it's what's running around in my head trying to find a way to burst out of my mouth.

Mum goes on, in a waspish sort of way, "Rosa, I SPECIFICALLY (yes, she really did say that in capital letters) I SPECIFICALLY asked you to take care of Alice yesterday at school. Megan tells me that Alice was quite alone in the playground. So where were you? I don't understand what you were thinking of."

Before I have a chance to respond, Megan The Old Friend Of The Family And Lying Cow says, "Oh, my dear, she was *far* too busy."

Far too busy? Now I'm the one who doesn't understand and I must look like an oxygen-deprived goldfish with my mouth flapping open and closed as I try to summon up some sort of suitable riposte. (To save you reaching for a dictionary - Riposte: A retaliatory retort, and I hope you know what retaliatory and retort mean otherwise I give up).

"Yes," says MTOFOTFALC (me abbreviating again) "She was far too busy…with…a young gentleman."

Whaaaaaaat? How dare she? Even Mum is surprised and says, "That doesn't sound like Rosa. It doesn't sound like Rosa at all."

Which makes me wonder what she's implying by that.

And I storm out of the kitchen before I have a chance to find out.

The kitchen seems to have become A Place To Storm Out Of, all of a sudden, or, if you want to be grammatically correct A Place Out Of Which To Storm but I thinks that sounds a bit up your own bottom.

Old friend of the family? I have far better ways of describing this woman which I won't write down here, in case of legal proceedings

Or a command to wash my mouth out with soap and water.

Chapter 14

With remarkable self-restraint, I let out my fury in the garden by decapitating dead roses and some live ones with well-aimed kicks from my trusty purple boots.

It's a good job flowers can't feel pain. I am absolutely sure about this and the little squeaking sounds must be coming from my own throat with the exertion of murdering Innocent Vegetation which is probably better than murdering A Lying Old Woman from the point of view of not going to prison.

After a while I sneak up to the window to see what's going on. Alice hasn't come out yet and, while I couldn't care less about school, if I have to go I'd rather arrive on time so as to be less noticeable. It's not that I'm a wimp but just have a strong sense of self-preservation and what's the point of deliberately drawing attention to yourself?

I might have thrown up when I look into the kitchen. Alice is sitting on her knee. Not her own knee which would be quite difficult, but on this Megan-biddy's knee. And Megan is pawing her and stroking her as though she were a pet Pekinese or another of those dogs that is more of a fashion accessory than an animal. And Alice is lapping it up which I suppose you would do if you were a Pekinese or similar. I mean to say, she's twelve years old! She's a human being! Admittedly, she's always been strange but this is going too far.

My tap on the window alerts Alice and she waves at me. Mum scowls and Megan licks her lips and gloats as if she's scored a little victory, which she has over decent behaviour for an adult with a twelve year old girl, in my opinion.

I should go inside and put a stop to it, really, but

something makes me hesitate, which is possibly cowardice.

Luckily, just then Alice comes trotting out of the door. Even more luckily she has my school bag as well as hers so I don't have to go back inside and be contaminated by unpleasantness. I nearly am though, because Mum and Megan follow her out.

Mum says, "Rosa..." firmly and then doesn't say anything else but I know that in those four letters of my name she is in fact saying, "Rosa if you don't look after your sister today you will be in serious trouble and by serious trouble I mean serious."

Megan says, "Have a lovely day at school, Alice." With emphasis on the word Alice so that she makes it plain that I'm not included in any pleasant wishes.

We head off down the lane.

"Megan's nice," says Alice.

I am lost for words.

I am lost for logical thoughts.

Again.

Chapter 15

I'm not talking to Alice as we go along the track by the woods, for reasons which must be obvious. If they're not obvious, it's because I'm completely and utterly fed up with her (but not even slightly jealous that she gets all the kindness and attention, so don't even think it).

My pace is so fast that she has to jog to keep up with me, but I won't slow down even though I'm making myself quite out of breath.

"I love you Rosa," pants Alice at one point, but I pretend not to hear. Then, presumably to amuse herself because it certainly isn't amusing me, she starts on her poetry again.

What tumbles out of her mouth are snatches of poems about trees and woods and forests. I know because I can't help listening and wondering how she does it. It's quite eerie really but the explanation may be that she's got a photographic memory and reads poetry books when no-one's watching. But I've never seen her. But if she only does it when no-one's watching then I wouldn't have done, would I?

Her voice is strange too, when she does the poetry thing. I mean, not her normal voice which is a normal voice. I don't quite know how to describe it but it's as though she's speaking through a wodge of cotton wool.

Wishing I hadn't walked so fast because my breath is getting jerky even though I try to control it, I'm stumbling over twigs and blades of grass and nothing at all because my legs are so exhausted. Alice doesn't stumble once. Her feet seem to have developed wings. Not literally, but now she flies along beside me with no effort which is majorly annoying like a lot of things about her.

Then suddenly she stops dead.

I carry on for a while but something makes me turn back. Alice faces towards the woods and her face is white and trembly as though she's just seen something unspeakable like maggots writhing in her dinner.

"What's wrong?" I shout, but she's miles away. Miles away in her head but only about three and a half yards from me in reality. I start to go back but it's like I'm someone wearing ten-ton concrete boots.

And she's chanting in her weird poetry voice, "I am prisoner, of the tree I am prisoner..."

Painfully, slowly I get closer to her shouting, "Alice, Alice what are you going on about?"

Out of the corner of my eye, I see deer zig-zagging through the woods and I hear birds squawking danger. And then Alice clutches at her throat as though she's being strangled. At the same moment there's a huge gust of wind that comes out of nowhere and an ancient tree crashes to the ground.

And so does Alice.

When I get to her she's all limp and her eyes are closed and I'm flapping about trying to remember Basic First Aid and rather hoping I won't have to do that mouth-to-mouth resuscitation thing.

I needn't have worried.

She opens her eyes at once and says with an angelic smile plastered all over her perfect angelic face, "Oops! I tripped over." Then she gets up and starts to brush down her immaculate school uniform which isn't very immaculate anymore and she looks at me with a puzzled frown crinkling her brow asking, "What's the matter Rosa?"

She's asking me what's the matter? Is she insane? Is insanity catching?

I don't think so but I'm beginning to wonder.

Chapter 16

The rest of the walk to school is deadly dull. Deadly dull is fine by me sometimes, although it doesn't give me much to write about. Oh, I do see Brother of GN by the school gate but I totally ignore him when he smiles at me, because I can see right through the smile to the scorn. He has very green eyes, which is quite unusual.

Double Maths lessons are worse than deadly dull, especially if you have to do simultaneous equations that you've already done years ago in your school in Notting Hill because the pupils there are so much more intellectually advanced. Looking on the bright side it means I won't have to work very hard here.

I'm sitting right in the middle of the class. This is a tactical manoeuvre. If I sit at the front people will think I'm a swotty teacher's pet and I can't sit at the back, which is where I'd like to be, because the whole row is occupied by GN and The Sycophants.

I'm in a sort of exclusion zone with the desks all round me empty. This is okay by me because it means I can't catch Intellectual Incapacity, which is rife in this place. (For your information, it's not actually catching any more than the insanity but you can't be too careful).

I sit upright and proud and pretend to be oblivious to the fact that screwed-up balls of paper keep hitting me on the back. Is that really the best they can do? Some of us grew out of playing silly games like that when we were about four years old in infant school.

The teacher drones algebra at the front of the room. "Drone, drone, drone, simultaneous equations are two equations with two unknowns, drone, drone. They are called simultaneous equations because…?"

Then he pauses and we're meant to finish the

sentence. Perhaps he doesn't actually know what simultaneous equations are and this is a clever strategy so that he can find out. To help you out if you don't know, the answer is... Because they must both be solved at the same time (I think).

He turns to the board and starts scribbling meaningless letters and numbers on it in illegible writing which would result in a detention if it were a pupil doing it. Another ball of paper hits the back of my neck and my ears burn as though they've gone bright red and they're filled with the sound of stupid feeble girly laughter. (Saying girly laughter is actually an insult to girls everywhere, so I apologise. Put it down to stress).

The teacher's drone continues..."The first step is to eliminate one of the unknowns..." And GN says, "Yeah, that's just what we're trying to do, sir," and she chucks another missile at me.

Aren't teachers paid to notice things like this?

I notice something.

I notice that my hands are clenched into fists under the desk and that I wish I had some more Innocent Vegetation to destroy.

Chapter 17

A couple of nights later and I'm happy to go to bed very early even if it's at the same time as Alice, in fact I would have gone even earlier than that given half a chance.

This is because Mum and Dad are having a Terrible Row and it's quite embarrassing to be anywhere near them. It's even quite embarrassing to be in our bedroom hearing angry sounds coming up through the floorboards.

Alice is lying flat on her back staring at the ceiling and she stretches out a hand towards mine and I take it (yes, our bedroom is that small) because I'd quite like to hold someone's hand too, even if it's only Alice's.

Parents must think their children are deaf and stupid. Do they seriously imagine that just because they go silent when we come into the room or pretend that they're having a civil conversation about the weather or the price of custard powder…do they seriously imagine that we are not aware that there is Something Very Amiss?

Part of me wants to find out what it's all about and part of me wants it to stop immediately. NOW as Mum would say. I'm Torn, Torn just like that song by Natalie Imbruglia she sometimes sings which I won't mention because it's not cool, even though quite good.

Little bits of what they, but mostly Mum, are yelling shoot upwards in jagged jets of anger which would be fiery red and deathly black jets if they were real and not just metaphors. Bits like this: "Tristan DeVere chinless wonder…Gloria jumped up American trollop…wanton destruction…golf complex…our natural heritage…several acres…kicking and screaming into the twenty-first century…progess…"

Some of the words I need to check in my dictionary and some of the other words wouldn't even appear in the dictionary because they are too offensive.

Alice's eyes are all shiny with tears so I squeeze her hand and she squeezes mine back and I realise she's not so bad after all and we are United In Distress.

I must have dropped off to sleep at some point because I wake up. There's still a rumbling coming from downstairs so I'd have preferred it if I hadn't made the mistake of waking up and I'm glad Alice hasn't.

Then I wake up again which is a bit of a mystery for someone who didn't actually fall asleep.

Silence.

Silence except for the sound of Alice breathing gently.

Silence except for another sound which is the stairs creaking as someone goes down them trying not to make them creak.

Silence except for the back door opening and closing again.

In fact it's hardly silent at all. It just seems quite silent after the horrendous noise of The Vicious Row.

I leap out of bed, as quietly as anyone could leap out of a rickety old bed, and rush to the window. The moon's being useful again because there's Mum, illuminated like a ballerina in a spotlight, dressed in an extraordinary black cape that reaches to the ground and swishes behind her as she makes her way across the lawn. And I don't have to tell you who is waiting for her under the yew tree. (Do I?)

Together they scurry off into the night.

That's it. I've had it up to here with all this secretive whispering-in-corners and acting-rather-oddly-for-a-grown-up business.

I'm going to find out exactly what's going on.

Chapter 18

I throw on some jeans and a hoodie to cover my face (the side bits not the front, otherwise I wouldn't be able to see anything). Alice is still asleep so I creep downstairs. Actually I creak downstairs but Dad's snoring is so loud it could have been a herd of rampaging water buffalo and no-one would have noticed.

Mum and Megan are out of sight but, after a quick sprint across the garden, there in the distance are two figures hurrying along the track towards the woods. The little hunched-up one carries one of those hurricane lanterns, which must be for effect as the moonlight is perfectly bright enough for most people who've got eyes.

It's quite easy to catch up with them and once I'm closer I keep right in to the hedge so as to be at least a little bit hidden from view in the shadows. The trouble is, it's annoyingly scratchy and my sleeves keep getting caught up in brambles, but you can't have everything.

It's all going very well then suddenly they take a sharp turn to the right and they're gone. Cursing under my breath like they do in Indiana Jones, I start running and quickly take back all my insults about the hurricane lantern. I would have lost them altogether if it hadn't been for its light, bobbing and flickering through the trees.

So this is Wayland Wood, is it? I'm not a great expert on woods but the trees seem awfully close together. They don't seem awfully close together ahead of me but if I look back they seem to have *moved* awfully close together so that the only way to go is forwards. I put it down to the effect of shadows but, even so, a prickly feeling trots up and down the back of my neck. I don't think this is ants.

After a while, the helpful light from the lantern isn't helpful any longer. Ahead, there's a circle of brightness and the sound of crackling flames and of weird chanting like Alice spouting poetry multiplied by a hundred, so even if it was pitch black I'd still be able to find my way.

Mum and Megan burst out of the darkness and fling off their capes and underneath they're wearing long white robes. Through the gaps between the trees I can see lots of other people wearing exactly the same and they're all dancing round a stone altar and I've never seen anything quite so idiotic in my entire life.

If only I'd brought a hankie to stuff into my mouth because I'm convinced I'll erupt in fits of uncontrollable laughter at any minute and then my presence would be discovered.

If only I'd brought a video camera as well. (Not to stuff into my mouth to stop the giggles, though it might have worked).

My mum seems to be in some sort of trance, writhing and groaning as if she's got indigestion from her own cooking, and I'm going to find it impossible to take her seriously ever again.

I creep right to the edge of the clearing, but still in the shadows, and peer round a gnarly old tree trunk for a good view of the whole freaky scene.

When I say freaky I mean freaky. I'm not exaggerating about this, honestly.

A masked woman, wearing not many skimpy clothes, clambers on to the altar so she'll probably catch pneumonia. Serves her right. But then again she might not because the next minute an extremely small man with striped black and white hair appears, who might be a dwarf but that's Politically Incorrect.

With a flaming torch almost as big as he is, he sets

light to a pile of sticks around the base of the altar and fire begins to lick at the woman's ankles so she could get scorched legs but she certainly won't get a chest infection through being too chilly.

OMG, a human sacrifice, is it? This is unexpected.

A doddery old man with one mad wandering eye scatters green flaky stuff to the winds. It looks like Dried Mixed Herbs from Sainsbury's but I could be mistaken. He's followed by a youngish man with ropey dreadlocks that tumble down to his bum, who rings a little brass bell at each corner of the altar.

And then there's a masked boy who could be about my age dressed up to look something like a tree, with the bare bits of his skin painted green. It's one thing adults making a fool of themselves like this, but someone my age should know better.

There's a moment when it looks like he's seen me, he stares so long in my direction, but I'm well-hidden so it's probably just that I'm beginning to feel uncomfortably like A Voyeur. Which I am. A Voyeur and uncomfortable.

There's one man who's way taller than everyone else and horribly emaciated with pointy shoulders and a knobbly sort of neck like a vulture. The wreath of oak leaves round his head give me a bit of a clue that he might be The King Of The Freaky People and that proves to be right when suddenly he booms, "Well met by moonlight!" as though he had invented the phrase when everyone knows it's nearly the same as one from *A Midsummer Night's Dream*. Then he says "Let the ritual commence!"

Let the ritual commence?

This is surely going to be worth watching.

Chapter 19

So I watch.

And it was (worth watching).

And I'm fascinated, transfixed, mesmerised and many other words with a similar meaning. And yes, I'm also uncomfortable. Not uncomfortable in the sense of getting cramp through staying in one position for too long, although that's a distinct possibility, but uncomfortable because this is private and I'm a spy and one of the people I'm spying on is my own mother (but I reckon she asked for it).

CRACK!

I nearly faint with shock at the snap of a twig and a sharp intake of breath behind a different dark tree to the left of me, followed by a rustling in the undergrowth.
    I can feel my heart bouncing round my chest and I think about bolting for home but just then The Ritual starts and I'm glued to my tree trunk in a mixture of amazement and disgust, which is a very sticky combination.
    There's smoke wafting all around the masked woman on the altar now the fire's died down a bit. Her legs don't appear to be even slightly singed so she can count herself lucky. She throws her head back raises her arms to the sky and lets out a heart-rending scream which makes me gasp but doesn't seem to bother anyone else.
    They all cluster round the altar faces shining with excitement – at least those that I can see are shining, including Mum's.

Then the woman starts a moaning, groaning chant in a false American accent like a wannabe film star but she doesn't fool me.

"Blessed child, for you my heart awaits.
Blessed child, for you my soul awaits.
Blessed child, for you my body awaits.
By Earth and Fire,
By Wind and Sea..."

And she sinks to her knees cradling an invisible baby in her arms, or that's what it looks like, and she finishes in almost a whisper but one of those penetrating whispers that can be heard about half a mile away.

"Born of my body you will be."

Then she crumples into a sobbing heap and so do I, nearly, but my sobbing is with laughter.

BOOM!

Another heart-lurching moment which serves me right for mocking the afflicted.

BOOM! and then more booms.

A swarthy man beats on a drum with a pounding rhythm and marches round the altar. They all follow him, chanting, and I think the chant's this though it's quite difficult to catch the words when it's a whole lot of people all at once.

"We call on thee, blessed child.
Come to her heart.
Come to her soul.
Come to her body.
Come! Come! Come!"

Then The King looks in a massive book as massive as the biggest encyclopaedia in the world which rests

on a stone plinth as there's no way he could lift it without a crane. In his echoey voice he reads, "Evocation of Brigit, protectoress of mothers and children, The Mystic Circle of the Young Girl!"
Megan suddenly comes to life and turn, eyes blazing, towards Mum, screeching just one word and that word is Alice.
WHAT?
And Mum looks a bit taken-aback and says, "Alice?"
Then they fall to their knees in complete silence.

If it hadn't been silent, I wouldn't have heard a suppressed snigger and a snort coming from the left of me as though someone was trying very hard not to explode.

If it hadn't been silent, they wouldn't have heard it either.

I didn't see him move, I swear I didn't, but without warning the King of the Freakies looms up a few feet from me bellowing, "An unbeliever in our midst! Show yourself or be damned!"
And before I have a chance to think what to do, Ginger Nut hurtles out of the undergrowth into the clearing and Freak King turns away from me and lunges towards her. I'm shaking and quaking now, to be truthful.

"Loser!" Ginger Nut spits at him making the sign with her thumb and forefinger. "You'd like a bit of a sight of me wouldn't you? In your dreams, pervert!"

Then she whips round and legs it back into the trees right past where I'm cowering like a gibbering idiot.

She's certainly got some guts. I'll give her that.

Chapter 20

I can't think of anything to do except follow her and as I'm stumbling away from the clearing the swarthy man yells, "I'll tan your hide when I catch up with you, Caitlin Wilding!"

And GN calls back over her shoulder, "Yeah Dad, whatever you say Dad," which makes me smile even though concentrating very hard on not tripping over branches or bumping into tree trunks.

Another man's voice thunders, "After her!" and behind us there's a crashing in the undergrowth and fearsome yelling but it soon tails off and rumbles to a halt.

I expect it's hard to give chase through the woods in the pitch black when you're an adult wearing fancy dress.

We keep running though, on parallel paths, me and Caitlin-formerly-known-as-Ginger-Nut. I can see her sometimes and sometimes I'm sure I glimpse A Third Person running in the same direction weaving between the trees the same as we are.

This Third Person looks fairly much like the medieval girl in my dreams so, unless it's one of the freaks I hadn't noticed, I must be hallucinating through lack of oxygen or not enough sleep or something. Yes, it's all in the mind, you idiot, Rosa. And so is the sound of the baby screaming. But it does make me run faster and the imaginary girl disappears and so does the screaming and then there's only me and Caitlin.

We reach the country track at almost the same moment as each other but quite a way apart.

If I was thinking that now I was safe from freaky people I was wrong.

Between us looms a huge shadowy giant of a man

absolutely enormous and terrifying. Most terrifying is that he's brandishing a shotgun which he points first at me and then at Caitlin and then back at me and he roars, "Oi! Trespassers will be prosecuted! Or shot!"

Then

KERBOOM!

He fires the shotgun into the air and I think I'm going to pass out and he shouts, "Let that be a warning to you!"

I hear Caitlin yelling "Tosser!" and we belt off in opposite directions, me wishing I could come up with good things to say to people in moments of extreme need instead of thinking of them ten minutes afterwards.

Chapter 21

I can hardly breathe, let alone stagger, when I get home, so it's quite a relief to open the garden gate and have only the lawn to crawl across before reaching the safety of the cottage. My mind's racing much faster than my legs ever have done, that's for sure.

Stretching out one exhausted hand for the back-door...

CRASH

It flies open in my face. I've had quite enough shocks for one evening without that and without Alice flinging herself into my arms sobbing and gulping, "You weren't here, Rosa, you weren't here, running through the trees I saw you and the baby's face like yours, and she's crying, crying..."

Uh? Is she psychic or something? She's clinging to me like velcro and I try to calm her down in my best big sistery way, patting her on the back and mumbling, "It's okay, Alice it's okay." But then I blow it by saying, "Well actually it's NOT okay because I think Mum's gone completely stark raving mad," which makes Alice cry all the more.

Good job, Rosa!

Sigh...

So then I have to practically carry her up the stairs to our bedroom and wrap her in a blanket which is what you do for People In A State Of Shock. (Perhaps I should wrap myself in a blanket, but since when did *I* matter?) You should also make them hot sweet tea but I can't be bothered.

If Dad wasn't snoring quite so loudly I'd go and tell him everything, but I'd need industrial-strength ear plugs just to go into the room so...perhaps tomorrow instead, when it might be a bit quieter?

It seems a bit disloyal to think of telling Dad what a flaky person Mum is and the strange things she gets up to, but it also seems a bit disloyal *not* to tell Dad what a flaky person Mum is and the strange things she gets up to.

Sometimes I think that children can't win. Sometimes I think that there must be advantages to having only one parent (not in the biological sense because that would be impossible).

I try to discuss things with Alice but her eyes have glazed over and she's muttering bits of verse so I shake her quite roughly by the shoulders and try to get her to snap her out of her ramblings.

"Alice, I need your help here," I say, but she quivers and curls up into a little ball.

Yes, go on Alice. Just disappear into La-La Land and let me do all the worrying, why don't you?

Chapter 22

Morning arrives very quickly which isn't that surprising as it was practically here already by the time I got in last night.

Oh, I had such a lot of sleep what with being in Wayland Woods for so long and then worrying myself silly about What To Do Next.

I heard Mum creep in about an hour after I did so she's going to be well-rested too, isn't she? But then she doesn't have to go to school, does she? And she didn't have to go out last night, whereas I felt I had to for the sake of the family.

Grown-ups have it so easy.

I know Dad is generally pretty useless but I'm still thinking he should know about last night. I need to tell someone at any rate because this stuff that's worrying me is too heavy to carry around in my brain all on my own.

But what to say? I compose a little speech in my head.

"Dad, not only have you a daughter who is away with the fairies but I am sorry to inform you that your wife is as mad as a bucket of frogs as well, which I don't expect you've noticed because you've been so busy wallowing in a morass of self-pity since you lost your job that you don't notice anything very much at all."

That should work. (Joke!)

Of course, me being such a pathetic light-weight, whatever it is I actually do say will be nothing like that at all.

I surprise even myself with my enthusiasm by getting ready for school extra early then lurk outside Mum and Dad's bedroom door waiting for The Right

Moment. A Moment arrives very quickly but it doesn't turn out to be The Right One.

Dad bursts through the door practically knocking me over because he's looking over his shoulder as he barges past me and into the bathroom and he's saying, "Well you've changed your tune a bit, Sal."

To avoid being trampled over a second time, I retreat and it also means I can listen to what they're saying without them realising. I needn't have bothered. Dad shouts this next bit so loud I expect they can hear it in Notting Hill.

"Yesterday they were Lord and Lady Muck, don't touch them with a ten foot barge pole, and now you want me to go round there with the girls!"

"Not the girls," says Mum, "Just Alice."

I'm not sure whether to be relieved or upset so I choose upset. Well actually, it chooses me.

Dad comes trundling out of the bathroom again as he's saying, "Just Alice? What the bloody hell is that all about?" Then he notices me and says, "Rosa!" his head lowered all embarrassed.

"Yes, that's me," I reply, "Rosa, the family freak who must be kept from public view." (so I *can* say clever things on the spur of the moment, sometimes!) I push past him and rage down the stairs but not loudly enough to drown out his voice which is saying, "Wrong time of the month is it? Bloody women."

Then I know I'll never tell him about Mum.

Then I know I'll never tell him anything ever again.

Chapter 23

"I didn't mean to upset you Rosa," says Mum, a bit later in the kitchen. She's plaiting Alice's hair and threading it with silly pink satin ribbons which will make her even more the subject of bullying but try telling Mum that.

I don't reply. Instead I stick a fork into my tights and watch the ladder shoot up my leg. She tries again in her wheedly I-really-care-about-you-Rosa voice, saying, "It was simply that I felt if we all went round to the DeVeres' it would be a bit, you know, overwhelming, and Gloria is Not Well."

Which doesn't fool me for a single second.

"Poor Gloria. Why is she not well?" asks Alice so sweetly that I could kick her if my leg would reach round the kitchen table as far as her shin.

"She is Having Trouble Conceiving," Mum says seriously, "And I think that we, as women, must show her our support, don't you girls?"

"Oh yes, Mummy," says Alice.

And I think I'm going to vomit into the pedal bin any minute.

"What's conceiving?" she adds.

Then a little light bulb flashes on in my brain (not literally) Of course! The masked woman on the altar. That must have been Gloria and that was what the ritual was all about. Perhaps. Maybe.

I expect anyone looking at me at this precise moment would be able see the cogs in my mind clicking round at high speed, not to mention the flashing light bulb.

"So…" I say grandly, about to make a revelation, but Mum interrupts.

"So…"she says, "I think we will *all* go round to

visit them this afternoon. Won't that be nice?"

I don't think it will be nice at all but I do think it will be Quite Interesting so my scowl is only half-hearted. Alice says, "But Daddy isn't a woman." Which is a fair point.

Annoyingly, Mum has an answer for everything and in this case it's, "But Daddy will keep Tristan occupied for us so we can talk about Important Female Matters."

Then she looks at me very oddly and adds, "Oh, by the way Rosa...about Caitlin Wilding..."

How does she know Caitlin?

"What about her?" I ask, suspicion welling up inside me.

Her eyes narrow and she says, "Don't believe everything she tells you. She's prone to..." She does one of her hesitations and I say, "She's prone to tell the truth, Unlike Some People Round Here?" in a voice that is meant to be pointed.

"No, she's prone to exaggerate," says Mum, then she looks away as though she's saying something uncomfortable and mutters, "As is her father. I don't want you listening to him either. Especially not about..." Then she stops.

"Especially not about what?"

A vivid redness shoots up her neck and bathes her face in an uncomfortable rosy glow.

"It doesn't matter. Just be wary of that...family."

Oh sure, right, well, I am SO convinced by what she's saying. Not.

What I say out loud is "Caitlin's cool."

"Yesterday you said she was an inbred mutant bitch," says Alice helpfully.

I could kill her. I think I will kill her because then she says, "Oh, and Mummy, Rosa wants to know what you were doing in the woods last night."

All cool now, redness retreating back down her

neck, Mum says, "In the woods? What are you talking about, Rosa? You must have been dreaming."

And this is the final nail in Alice's coffin, the sneaky little grass.

"You see, Rosa," she says, "Mum's not going completely stark raving mad after all."

Chapter 24

If Alice thinks I'm going to walk her to school she's got another think coming. I am furious with her plus lots of expletives. And if Mum thinks I'm going to walk Alice to school then tough titty because I'd rather gouge my eyes out with a teaspoon.

I can walk very fast when angry and today I'm supercharged. Perhaps Britain could employ this tactic in the Olympic Games - make the athletes extremely cross and then they'll be so hyper they'll win loads of gold medals.

Yes, it's a rubbish idea but don't bother telling me it is, because I may lash you with my venomous tongue, which is a fancy way of saying I'll swear vilely at you.

I AM ON THE POINT OF EXPLODING WITH FURY.

Behind me on the track, Alice tries in vain to catch up with me. I can hear little snatches of that nauseating, babyish rhyme, "My mother *said* I never *should*, Play with the *gyp*sies in the *wood*."

I turn round and scream louder than my throat finds comfortable, "Shut UP, Alice!"

She doesn't.

"*Naught*y little girl to *dis-o-bey*..."

I do that thing of putting my fingers in my ears and going la-la-la very loudly just to block out her reedy little voice before I go completely ape.

The next time I look round she's disappeared.

GOOD!

After that, my walk to school is quite pleasant apart from the bit where I step in a splurgy cow pat.

Who should be waiting at the gate for me but Caitlin, minus the sycophants, thank goodness, and I give her a wary kind of half wave. And, of course, completely ignore anything Mum said earlier.

Funny thing is, Caitlin's shortened her skirt and knotted her tie just like mine. Rosa the fashionista! The girls at my old school would wet themselves laughing at the very idea because I was always considered to be the Height of Not Cool.

Caitlin sidles up to me, not the least bit cocky like before, and asks "Did Alice stay at home today then?"

"She's on her way," I reply and add, "She pisses me off."

Caitlin is the first person I've ever admitted that to apart from Jules and it's a bit of a relief when she says, "Yeah, she's certainly a bit…different."

"Last night?" I begin.

Caitlin smiles. "Yeah, saw you there. It's better than telly, watching that."

"Do you really think so? I think it's weird."

"Nah!" she says. "Makes me laugh."

Perhaps Caitlin's right. That's a less unsettling way to look at it than filling my head with worries about Family Insanity and Will I Be Next? In fact, before it got a bit heavy with the chase through the woods and everything I was laughing myself, wasn't I? Or, at least, trying to stop myself from laughing. I should chill a bit more, really.

"Was that your dad then?" I ask.

"Yup. Keeps him out of the pub," she says.

"Mum said I must have been dreaming."

Caitlin laughs. "My dad tried that one too," she says. "Only the once, mind you! Parents? Who'd have 'em?"

And I laugh too. Caitlin's okay, really.

Then I remember Alice. Where the hell is she?

Chapter 25

Caitlin goes racing one way round the school and I go the other, not racing but sauntering, looking from left to right, I'm so used to this sort of thing happening with Alice. Once most of the possible hiding places have been eliminated, I break into a bit of a trot, fuelled by growing anxiety, not anger this time, too worried even to think about adding it to my Olympic gold medal strategy list.

Back in the playground now, Caitlin sprints up to me saying that no-one's seen Alice this morning, no-one at all, and she thinks with the way Alice looks people would remember if they had.

Shit.

Anger and guilt bubble up inside me and explode outwards in an invisible whoosh all over Caitlin's brother who arrives just at that moment and asks quite kindly if we need any help.

"What makes you think I could possibly need your help?"

It's exactly as if it's my mouth working on its own with no instructions from me because I didn't mean to say that at all.

Caitlin looks a bit put out and he shrugs and walks off again and I wheel round and round like a dying spinning top which isn't ever so helpful and it's a good job Caitlin's there to take charge. She pulls me by the arm saying, "Come on, Rosa! Let's go back the way you came. Hurry!"

And still I'm flapping round in circles of indecision and a large part of me is muttering to itself, "She'll turn up, she always does."

It isn't until Caitlin says, "Rosa, please...The game-keeper..." that I do move. In fact I've never moved so fast in all my life. (I should bear that in mind for the hundred metres).

Chapter 26

We scurry along the track calling out Alice's name every so often just in case she's wandering about somewhere out of our sight. Once or twice, I'm sure I hear her answering in an echoey voice, "Rosa, I'm here, I'm here," but we stop to listen, call again and – nothing.

Nothing.

The main thought that's running through my mind is that Mum will kill me, she'll utterly kill me, which I suppose is a bit on the selfish side (I mean, me thinking of myself is a bit selfish not Mum killing me. That would be extremely selfish).

The edge of the woods is like a solid black wall as though the trees have closed ranks to prevent any intruders from getting in. There's no way we can see into its depths even though it's broad daylight. I was certain I'd recognise the gap I went through last night but there is no gap.

Caitlin and I don't say anything to each other. I had the thought that if we said out loud what we were thinking it might make it come true so it's better not to. We trudge on, sometimes running mostly walking.

Then, in the distance, we see someone on the track only he doesn't seem very distant at all because he's so huge. Wheeling around his legs are two massive black dogs. Even from here I can see them slavering and hear their growls.

Caitlin whispers, "Oh no, Bates the game-keeper." And her voice is filled with panic.

I look at Caitlin and she looks at me and we still don't say anything because we don't need to. We just break into a run and as we do Alice appears out of the woods, between us and Bates, with Megan at her side. I think I screamed her name.

"Go get 'em, boys," roars Bates, and the dogs launch into a ferocious attack and now everything happens very quickly but it's in slow-motion at the same time if that makes any sense, which I don't suppose it does.

We're still hurtling along trying to get to Alice when Megan darts behind a tree, the complete and utter coward, leaving Alice to face the dogs alone. But then the hare shoots out from the undergrowth nearby and the dogs catch its scent and right at the very last minute they veer away from Alice and after it instead, disappearing into the heart of Wayland Woods.

I get to Alice and scoop her up into my arms, amazed that the only thing she's crying is, "Megan, where's Megan?"

Doesn't she realise that Megan abandoned her to A Horrible Fate? And what was she doing with Alice in the woods anyway? You hear stories about people like Megan, only usually they're about middle-aged men in dirty raincoats.

Caitlin throws herself at Bates, pounding her fists on his chest and screaming, "You bastard, you bloody bastard, you should be locked up."

I wish I had half her nerve.

And Bates laughs. Can you believe it? He laughs and then he growls a deep rumbly growl, "These here woods are private, part of the DeVere estate. It's my job to stop trespassers."

He sticks two fingers in each corner of his mouth and lets out an ear-splitting whistle, one of those ones you try for hours to do but you only manage a spluttery squeak.

The two dogs appear again in an instant, no hare and certainly no Megan clenched between their evil teeth. Actually, close up they're quite sweet and wag their tails a lot even though they must have been trained to be Fierce Killing Machines.

"Megan!" squeals Alice in delight and there she is, slinking out from behind a tree. The dogs yelp oddly at the sight of her and retreat behind Bates' legs and I feel like doing the same because that old woman really gives me the creeps. That's not to say I want to yelp and retreat behind Bates' legs, in case you're worried (that would be gross) but just retreat as far away from Megan as possible. Alice, on the other hand, rushes over to her and gives her a hug. Caitlin and I exchange disgusted glances.

One arm round Alice, Megan sneers at Bates, "Call yourself a man? Begone! And take your craven hounds with you. The DeVeres shall hear of this!"

Which is quite an impressive speech, I have to admit.

"You can be sure the DeVeres will hear of this," says Bates, obviously a lot less impressed than I am.

He marches off, dogs cringing at his heels.

Chapter 27

So there we are, me, Caitlin, Alice and Megan, standing on the edge of Wayland Woods, no-one quite knowing what to say or do next. I'm boiling up inside like a pressure cooker but it's Megan who speaks first, saying, "Well girls…" in that cackly voice of hers that reminds me of a witch in a fairytale.

The pressure cooker inside me blows.

I lunge towards her. She's such a wizened old crone that I have to crouch down to get my face level with hers. "It's you, isn't it?" I snarl. (It probably wasn't much of a snarl but it's a good word to describe how I wanted to sound).

Alice jumps between us begging me to leave Megan alone but I'm unstoppable now, nearly. I snarl some more. "You're the one who lurks round the house and waits for my mother in the dead of night, aren't you?"

Caitlin wades in right beside me saying, "Yeah, she's One Of Them, alright."

"Don't say those horrible things," says Alice, and starts to cry.

"More things in heaven and earth, Rosa, than are dreamt of in your philosophy," hisses Megan unoriginally. (I suppose she thinks I haven't read *Hamlet*. Well, she's wrong).

I can't bear this for a second longer. I'm so riled that I'm shaking from top to toe and I can hear my voice rising about three octaves as I shriek, "It's like a nightmare, this is. It's like I say something perfectly sensible to people and I might as well be speaking Swahili."

Alice has stopped crying. She looks at me all innocent and announces, "This calls for the mad demon of poetry running barefoot over the coals, peeling back the truth…"

SLAP

I slap her.

Right across her perfect little face with my hand. In the shocked silence that follows, an angry red mark intensifies on her cheek.

Chapter 28

I think I must have deleted the next few minutes from my memory. Actually, that's a lie. It's just that I don't want to write about it.

Sooooooo...

A little later, Alice and Megan walk ahead along the track towards school. Caitlin stays beside me though I can't think why she'd want to. Every ten seconds (well, it seems that often) Alice turns round and looks straight at me and I don't look back, suddenly very interested in the earth beneath my feet and my left bootlace and odd bits of gravel and anything else that means I don't have to meet Alice's gaze.

I've never been so ashamed in my entire life.

Eventually I say to Caitlin, "I can't go to school, I just can't."

"I wouldn't worry about it," she replies. "Alice is cool. Amazing really. That was quite a thwack you gave her."

"Please, Caitlin, don't."

If I could shrivel any further into the ground and crawl under the nearest rock I would.

"We could bunk off, go to my place if you like," she suggests. All I can do is nod dumbly.

"Hang on a minute then," she says. "I'll ask Alice to tell Kieron where we are," and she races off. For a bit of a rebel she can be surprisingly mature sometimes. I wouldn't have thought of doing that in a million years. She must care about him. Someone has to.

I lean up against a tree and pick my nails until they bleed. So her brother's name is Kieron, is it? The Wildings must be a family that specialise in Unusual Names For Babies. They've probably got one of those books.

At one point I glance up and Alice is waving at me. She's smiling. How can she be smiling? Then Megan takes her hand and they set off again and Caitlin jogs back towards me.

"That's okay then," she says.

This might sound over-dramatic but I can't imagine how anything can ever be okay ever again, Ever. Yes, it does sound over-dramatic but when you've just seriously assaulted your kid sister and are writhing in terminal guilt and shame, you're allowed to be over-dramatic.

Caitlin takes me by the arm like I'm an invalid, which in many ways I am, and pulls me gently along a different track that cuts through the fringes of Wayland Woods.

I don't say a word for the next half hour but she chats without pausing for breath which helps a little bit to fill the huge hole that's gaping in my heart.

Chapter 29

Wayland Woods has multiple personalities, I'm beginning to realise. The part we're wandering through is almost pretty and the trees aren't gnarly and menacing at all. Here, now, the leaves rustle in a comforting way and, between them, dapply sunshine ripples down from the sky and I can't help feeling a tiny bit poetic.

If you don't know what that feels like then I expect you're A Philistine. I looked it up to be sure I wasn't being A Philistine myself by using the wrong word. It means: A person who is said to despise or undervalue art, beauty, intellectual content, or spiritual values. So that's not me. Obviously.

And it's not Alice either but I'm trying not to think about her.

My first sight of Caitlin's cottage is a plume of smoke curling upwards above the trees, although, if you want to be picky, that's not strictly part of the cottage.

My next sight is of a miniscule ramshackle shed-like thing that looks as though it might fall over sideways if you leant on it too hard. It has one of those crooked chimneys straight out of Hansel and Gretel and all around the outside there's clutter and junk and bits of rusty old cars and chickens pecking in the dirt. There's a lot of dirt. Dead birds hang in the porch like gruesome wind chimes and a queasy sensation rises up in my stomach.

I try very hard not to let any of the unsavoury thoughts show themselves on my face but I'm hopeless at hiding things (apart from my birthmark). Caitlin gives me a sideways glance and there's hurt in her eyes.

Why, oh why am I such a bitch?

We wander up the garden path, me trying not to stare at the squalor all around me. I haven't talked for so long that when I do it comes out all croaky.

"Won't your Mum be…?" I was going to say, furious we've skipped school or something like that but Caitlin cuts me short before I have time to think of the right words.

"She left," she says.

I can almost see the shutters come down around her. I say, "She left? That sucks."

"No, it doesn't suck," she mutters. "She's a slag and I hate her."

Then the door bursts open and there he is, The swarthy man from the other night bellowing, "Caitlin, you get your arse back to…" then he notices me and his swarthy face goes pale as though he's seen a ghost and he says, "Holy Shit." Then he says "Who the F…?" but Caitlin interrupts before he has a chance to use another obscenity.

"Haven't you got rabbits to skin or something?" she says.

This man, formerly known as swarthy who is now pasty white, remains there with his mouth drooping open so far I can practically see his tonsils. I thought people turning white only happened in sappy novels but believe me, I saw it with my own eyes and his eyes are all bulging and fixed on me so it's extremely squirm-making.

"Dad, you freak! Stop staring at her will you?" says Caitlin and grabs my sleeve and pulls me past him into the kitchen.

Then she slams the door behind us and shouts through it, "How sad can you get?"

Chapter 30

The kitchen is Something Else. Something Else that could make me say my mouth dropped open when I saw it if I hadn't decided never to use that phrase again. At least it takes my mind off being ogled by my best friend's dad.

I don't even know how to start describing it. The kitchen that is, not being ogled. By the way, I'm not famous for being ultra-tidy or even particularly clean (I'm fourteen) but I can honestly say I've never seen anything like this. Dirty dishes all furry with blue and green mould teeter in piles on every surface, foul greyish underpants and vests dry on chair backs, the windows are so grimy you wouldn't ever need curtains, the floor is covered with Animal Unmentionables and I can't go on writing this without reaching for a sick bag. (I really hope you aren't eating your dinner). It's squalid, very squalid, and squalid has just been promoted to my Word Of The Day.

Caitlin shuffles her feet and I don't know what to say. She does though and, with an apologetic half-smile, announces, "The cleaning lady doesn't come on Tuesdays."

"You have a cleaning lady?" I kind of splutter in a way that's meant to sound polite.

"Yeah, right," she says, and then, "Do you want a drink of something?"

"It's okay thanks I'm not thirsty," I say quickly. But inside I'm screaming, no way. My screaming inside must have sneakily found its way outside somehow.

"You won't catch anything," she says, "Only bubonic plague, maybe."

You have to admire her. Well, I do anyway. I smile at her and she smiles back.

"On second thoughts, could I have a cup of coffee?"

"Right," she replies, "I'll just have to go and grind a few acorns then, won't I?" and she grabs a jar of instant from the shelf.

Ha-di-ha-di-ha!

We have a lovely day after that sticky start (not referring to the kitchen floor again but to the embarrassing atmosphere)

Until she spoils it…

Chapter 31

By the afternoon we're sun-sozzled and drowsy, lying on a tartan rug under an apple tree with a jug of lemonade and the buzzy sound of insects lulling us off to sleep.

When my eyelids don't get so heavy that they close over my eyeballs I'm reading my copy of *Cider With Rosie*. I could be a character in that novel right at this very moment. It's a bit like reading the story of Apollo 13 when you're actually in a spaceship. Only better, because sci-fi is mostly for boys.

I don't think I've felt so relaxed for centuries and all the horrible Alice happenings of earlier have faded into nothingness. Then Caitlin has to go and remind me.

She has a funny little gold wristwatch which is so small you need a microscope to see the time on it but she says it was her mum's so that's why she wears it. That's funny, I think. She said she hated her mum, so why would she want to wear her watch? I don't say that to *her* though because I've got tact. Anyway, she peers at the tiny dial and tells me it's just gone three, as if I might be interested.

When I don't respond at all she says, "Don't you think we should..?" Then she stops awkwardly.

"Don't you think we should stay here?" I say, and turn over to page 73 of *Cider With Rosie*. (I've been drowsing over page 72 for the last half hour).

"I wasn't going to say that," she says. I know perfectly well what she was going to say. She was going to say didn't I think that we should collect Alice from school? I don't want to collect Alice. I don't ever want to see Alice again, preferably, so I say stuffily, "I'd rather not."

"Up to you," she replies. "She's your sister."

"Thanks for reminding me, Caitlin. Yes, it is up to me."

But after that I can feel disapproving eyes boring into my skull and I can't enjoy my book anymore. I sit up all hunched over myself to make it very clear I Am Not Amused.

"I was only saying," she says lamely.

"Well, stop saying," I snap. "It's none of your business so just back off."

So she does.

She goes into the cottage and leaves me in my strop. That's another reason for me to feel guilty today but not nearly as serious as the first reason, I can't help thinking.

It's only a couple of minutes later she comes running out of the door again followed by her dad who's shouting, "How many times have I got to tell you before you get it into your thick head, I don't want that effing girl in my house."

Which I suppose must mean me. Leaping to my feet I snatch up all my things and Caitlin cries out, "Rosa, where are you going?"

"Anywhere but here."

I stomp off along the path.

Caitlin bursts into tears but I don't turn back. I can hear her sobbing, "Sometimes I really wish Mum was still here."

I still don't turn back.

Then I think I hear her dad crying too which seems unlikely but I catch fragments of him saying, "So do I, sweetheart. So do I. But this place isn't... we aren't good enough for her now."

The last thing I hear, which I hear properly because I'm meant to hear it, is Caitlin calling out, "And I thought Rosa was nice."

Well, I'm not nice, am I?

I'm very far from being nice.

Chapter 32

No, I'm definitely not nice.

I'm a brat. A nasty, unpleasant, moody, selfish brat and I don't want to admit it, although I suppose by writing that I just did. The difficulty is, once you've backed yourself into that sort of corner, how do you get out of it? Because I'm so bratty at the moment, so full of anger, the thought of saying sorry to Caitlin and to Alice doesn't actually occur to me. If I were to look back in a few days time, I might be able to see that all my anger is directed at me but at the moment I think everything is their fault. Well, it is, isn't it?

I'm In Denial, you see. That is psychological stuff and thought up by a man called Freud, pronounced Froid unless you're French when froid means cold but isn't pronounced the same. It's when a person is faced with something that is too uncomfortable to accept so pretends it's not happening despite overwhelming evidence that it *is* happening. Mum does that quite a bit, as I've already said, so perhaps it's in my genes. (Read *The Complete Works Of Rosa Cavanagh* and learn interesting things. Maybe).

So, in this state of denial, I'm marching along raging about the unfairness of life and how hateful everyone is and how I wish I'd never come down to this stinking hole of a place and while raging I cover a surprising amount of ground and find myself beside a river.

It's lovely here. It's really lovely. I astonish myself by thinking that in the middle of all my crossness but there you go…out of my control.

The meadow is the greenest of greens, dancing with golden buttercups and little nodding daisies. The dizzying heat of the sun beats down on my head, but the river looks cool and clear and inviting, shimmering with glinty emerald and silver ripples.

And then, then, as I'm staring down into the delicious coolness of the river, I see her. A girl. Her naked body tangled in the reeds. Just for the tiniest part of a second, I see her, then I blink and there's nothing there.

I'm suffering from sun-stroke, probably.

With all my raging I've made myself horribly sweaty, as well. The water's calling to me, dark and deep.

Admittedly, I check all around me and there's no-one in sight and I can see for miles in every direction (every direction but one, as it turns out) but even so, for me to take my clothes off in a Public Place is unheard of. Except I'm convinced it's not a Public Place so it doesn't count.

Leaving everything in a jumbled heap, I slither down the grassy bank and into the water and after the initial I'm-going-to-have-a-heart-attack-it's-so-cold moment it's bliss and heaven all rolled into one, almost as good as swimming in the sea. Probably even better because there are no jelly-fish.

Perhaps I was a mermaid in another life? I could have been. I swim like one today and every bit of anger and every bit of resentment washes away in the gentle current. With a kick of my feet, I dive under. The water closes over me and I'm in a muffled opaque world of darting fish and wavering weeds.

For a moment, slimy tendrils tangle round my ankles but I thrash free and surface in a cascade of silver droplets and shake my head like a dog after an unwelcome bath.

It's then I hear the voices.

Chapter 33

The voices aren't talking, they're giggling and my heart would sink into my boots if I was wearing any because such giggles can only come from The Sycophants or similar and here I am skinny-dipping in a river and who knows how much the water has washed away the make-up on my face?

I glide silently to the bank and pull myself up inch by inch so I can just see over the edge. Then my heart gasps or perhaps it's my lungs or mouth because sure enough there are three Sycophants ambling along towards me chattering like magpies. To my utter gulping horror, a few paces in front of them is Kieron.

Shit. And double shit.

My clothes are too far away to reach and, anyway, I couldn't get them on without being seen so I look around frantically and then slide back into the water and swim as splashlessly as I can manage in my panic to an overhanging tree. A weeping willow. How very appropriate.

In the shadows made by the branches, and not having a periscope to hand, very carefully and cautiously I raise my head just above the water so I'm able to see across to the far bank. There's Kieron meandering along so laid back he's in danger of sliding into the river. The Silly Sycophants trot after him with their tongues hanging out.

And I expect I resemble a lurking crocodile, or more likely a hippopotamus.

"Hey!" exclaims Kieron and I know he's practically tripped over my clothes and I think I'll die at the thought of him seeing my knickers. He shades his eyes from the glaring sun with one hand and gazes up and down the river bank.

By this time The Sycophants have caught up with him. What happens next is like an episode from Sycophants Behaving Badly which is an idea I have for a TV comedy only at the moment I can't see the funny side of it.

The Sycophants gather round my pile of clothes and pick them up one-by-one between their fingers and thumbs, their mouths twisted into sneers of derision, the bitches. The posh-looking one twirls my bra in the air. It's from Marks and Spencer and I wouldn't be seen dead in it if I had the choice.

Posh Sycophant: "Oh. My. God. Look at this!"

Dumpy Sycophant: "Gross!"

"Grow up, will you?" says Kieron.

Spotty Sycophant: "I know who these belong to."

Kieron asks, "Who's that?"

"That stupid tart from London."

"Rosa, you mean?" Kieron stares at my bra. Shall I drown myself now or wait until my humiliation is complete?

The Posh One has a hold of my skirt. "She's so up herself." She drops it into the river. "Ooops, silly me!"

Dumpy and Spotty giggle helplessly like the brainless numpties they are. I contemplate bursting out of the river and smacking their stupid faces flat but my sense of dignity won't let me. Which is me kidding myself. It's just fear.

Kieron strides further along the river bank, hand still shading eyes from the water's glare as he searches for me. Presumably me. He looks concerned. Perhaps it's the Marks and Spencer bra.

I retreat further into the darkness. This is metaphorical as well as literal because of what happens next.

The Sycophants throw my clothes into the river, one article at a time.

"Tragic!" says Dumpy

"What if they sink?" says Posh

"What if they shrink?" says Spotty

Hoots of immature laughter. I'm kind of relieved when my knickers disappear under the water. They come from Marks and Spencer too.

Kieron turns back towards the Sycophants, his face scrunched up with disgust, "You morons!"

"Ooooh! Be like that!" squeals Posh, and Dumpy flounces, "See if we care!"

Kieron paces up and down the river bank, muttering just loud enough for me to hear. "Where the hell is she?" I bite down on my hand hard to stop any pathetic words coming out of my mouth.

"Come on girls. This is getting boring," drawls Spotty and sets off across the field.

Dumpy calls after her, "Don't we want to see her?"

"Crawling butt-naked out of the mud?" adds Posh.

Spotty doesn't look back. "Gross. I'd rather die."

Posh and Dumpy lollop after her, the three of them link arms and swagger off, laughing. It's a sound that's like a thousand needles piercing my heart.

Now what?

Kieron leans over the river bank and rescues my dripping shirt from the water. I'm thankful it's not my knickers. Or my bra. Suddenly he notices something in amongst the reeds.

"Christ!"

He dives into the water, searches frantically, splashily, in the depths, comes up for air, gulping painfully.

Then he dives down again.

For what seems to be a very long time.

Chapter 34

I can't let him carry on searching for me under the water. Apart from anything else, it doesn't look as though he's a very strong swimmer and there's quite enough on my conscience already today without being responsible for The Drowning Of An Incompetent Would-Be Rescuer.

Sliding out from under the shade of the willow tree, I tread water half way across the river. The next time he comes up for air, ladybird red in the face but without the black spots, I enquire politely, "What are you doing?"

Spluttering and coughing, he just about manages to gasp, "I thought you were tangled in the weeds…you…you watched me trying to…do that? You cow."

Then he flings himself towards the bank and drags himself out of the river, water streaming from his clothes, his hair, all of him.

"Wetting yourself laughing at me, were you?" he snaps, green eyes full of bitterness.

"No, not at all," I say feebly

Then he looks at me strangely and says "And those marks on your face…"

My hand shoots to my cheek then I check my palm. Crap. It's covered in splotchy beigey-orangey make-up.

"Serves you bloody well right," he finishes.

Then he marches off across the meadow, dripping half the contents of the river on the grass as he goes, and I hear him shout back over his shoulder, "Get your own sodding clothes."

Did he mean sodden or sodding? Or both?

I put both hands to my face this time and sink slowly under the water, wanting to stay there forever

85

but there's this thing called Buoyancy and there's also this thing called People Not Being Able To Breathe Under Water - so after about ten miserable seconds I rise to the surface in a maelstrom of bubbles and wonder if I'd have the courage of Virginia Woolf who drowned herself in a river weighted down with pebbles in her coat pockets but I haven't got any pebbles and am not wearing a coat and, being naked, have no pockets either... so I think probably not at the moment.

Chapter 35

Out of the water but in the depths of despair, I wring out my clothes and force them on to my body. It's not easy. It's a struggle. It makes my skin sore. My body shivers despite the sun beating down on it. It must be upset. I know my mind is.

One of my boots is missing. I look around vaguely for a while then see it. It's out of my reach, resting on its side on the sandy bottom of the river, little fish swimming in and out of it. I don't go back into the water...haven't the heart for it...don't know where to go. The only place I can think of is the home that isn't my home where at least I could hide in my half-bedroom until the world comes to an end then no-one will notice that mine has already.

I set off limping, one boot on, knowing it must make me look even more ridiculous than I am already but I'm past caring. My mind goes into a whirlpool state and it's scary.

There's a song Dad sometimes plays and I hate the lyrics and they snatch at my brain with needle teeth and claws and they won't let go until I'm screaming "Shut Up Shut Up Shut Up" with my hands over my ears and they go on and on, *And they saw birthmarks all over her body She couldn't quite explain it They'd always just been there,* on and on and on and in my mind I could see myself and then I'm in the photo and I'm my Auntie Deborah and then I'm the medieval girl in my dreams and then I'm the squalling baby and then I'm me again and it's a nightmare but I'm awake and running across the fields in one boot and all my clothes wringing wet and I'm crying like a baby, like that baby, and then I fall over and then I scrabble back to my feet again and I'm in a field of wheat that reaches to my waist and I'm a tiny lost figure in the vastness and in the distance there's a tractor spraying the crops and part of me wishes it would spray me so I'd shrivel up like a weed and the wheat swishes making a sound between sighing and gasping and the song goes on and on and on and then I see home and then I see Alice and she runs to me and hugs me and I'm saying, "I'm sorry, I'm sorry, I'm so sorry," and she's saying, "It doesn't matter Rosa, as long as you're safe."

And then the nightmare stops.

Chapter 36

"Rosa, what happened to you," says Alice. "You look half drowned. And where's your boot?" Then I mutter, "It doesn't matter," as well, and she says, "But your face…"

I say, less shakily this time, "I said it doesn't matter." and then, "Alice, I've got to get out of here. Will you help me?"

And her eyes fill with tears but she doesn't ask any questions.

She just says "Yes."

Chapter 37

I can hear Alice talking to Mum as I'm in the bedroom stuffing random clothes into a back-pack. Alice doesn't usually talk very much to anyone but me unless it's weird stuff, so I could hug her to bits for making such an effort to cover for me.

You should have seen Mum's face when I staggered into the kitchen just now but I didn't stop long enough to listen to her expressions of shock-horror-dismay.

"Hi," I said, barely glancing in her direction, head bowed to disguise the carnage, shot up the stairs into the bedroom, shut the door behind me, and slumped to the floor, safe at last.

Alice is saying fast and squeaky, "I'm telling you, Mum, we had a lovely day at school. Lovely! It was just, on the way home, we were larking about by the river and she tripped and... SPLASH!"

"But where exactly by the river?" says Mum insistently, as though it was an important detail and Alice remembers at least some of what I'd told her and proclaims, "There is a willow grows aslant the brook..." which if you don't know is the bit from Hamlet about Ophelia drowning herself and I think that's pretty spooky and so does Mum, it seems, because she lets out a gasp that I can hear right through the floorboards and screams, "Oh, dear God."

Then I hear her pounding up the stairs so I shove the back-pack under my bed before she bursts into the room and flings her arms around me as though I've escaped A Fate Worse Than Death when as far as she knows all that's happened is that I've fallen into a river and lost one of my boots. Weird. Very weird.

Weirdest of all is to be showered with tearful kisses by a mum who hardly ever notices my existence unless

I've done something wrong which is, as far as she's concerned, about once every ten minutes.

"Gerroff me," I say after a while, because it's unnatural.

"Oh Rosa," she says, "I was so worried about you."

Well, that's a lie for a start. She found out about The River Incident (the adapted version, at least) no more than half an hour ago.

"Anyway," she says, "You just make yourself look presentable now, darling. Don't forget we're going round to the DeVeres' for tea."

I protest and argue and those are my specialist subjects but I think my powers of resistance must have been weakened by what happened earlier.

That was very short-lived then, my mother actually caring about me and my feelings.

The Great Escape will have to be postponed.

Chapter 38

After a bit, I trundle resentfully downstairs in clean dry clothes, make-up repaired.

Mum and Dad are arguing in the garden, their favourite hobby. Alice sits at the kitchen table, doodling on a scrap of paper. I kiss her on top of her head and that is about as unusual as Mum slobbering all over me, but the difference is that I really mean it. She tilts her face sideways and smiles up at me and there's not a horrible slap mark on her cheek which I should have noticed earlier but I was too upset.

So that's good.

Then I glance down at her drawing and my heart does a somersault when I see that she's drawn my boot, lying at exactly the same angle as I left it on the river bottom, little fish swimming in and out of it.

"Alice?" I say with a huge question mark after her name.

"What?" she replies, then gazes down at the drawing, knowing somehow that it was what I was talking about.

"I saw it in my head," she says.

Then she pulls a tattered exercise book out of her school bag and tells me she's writing something especially for me and it's Very Important but she hasn't finished it yet.

"What it is?"

"It's your story, Rosa."

"My story?"

Hang on a minute, I'm writing my story, aren't I? Or so I thought.

"These are the bits you don't know about yet," she says, before my thoughts have a chance to be formed into speech.

And then she says, "Megan's helping me."

A black cloud passes over my mind.

"Alice," I begin, but the screams and shouts from the garden drown me out and we both run outside.

Strapped to his back, Dad has a huge metal drum with a skull-and-crossbones painted on it and the words POISON and WEED KILLER written large and ominous. In one hand he clutches a gun-thing and sprays foamy stuff wildly all around the tangled jungle that Mum likes to call a flowerbed. With the other hand he's fending her off as she struggles to wrestle the spray from his grasp.

She's screaming, "Keith, Keith, what are you doing?"

Does she really need to ask him? It seems quite obvious to me.

"I'm gardening," he bellows back at her, narrowly missing her with a great swoosh of spray.

"Raping Mother Nature you mean, don't you?" she screeches.

Then I notice Megan, bent double and spluttering on the other side of the fence - but she's miles away from Dad and his spray so that can't be anything to do with it.

Alice lets out a high-pitched wail and runs to Megan's side and it's enough to put a stop to Mum and Dad's stunning display of marital harmony, which is me being ironic in case you hadn't gathered.

Get involved? Me? No.

Mum and Alice are fawning all over Megan who has recovered in an instant so I reckon she was putting it on. Dad is scowling like a bad-tempered school-boy, hands in pockets, outside the shed where Mum has made him lock away the weed-killer. NOW!

"You were happy enough to use it in London," he barks at her, vicious as a rabid dog.

"Things are different here," she replies.

Don't I know it!

As I watch, the plants in Mum's flowerbed writhe and coil in agonizing death throes.

And Megan looks over at me with a glint in her eye, one corner of her mouth curled into a sneer.

Chapter 39

And here we all are now, about an hour later, The Happy Family Cavanagh, outside the DeVeres' residence. It's almost more than I can bear, but as long as we leave in time for me to catch the last train out of Nowhere to Somewhere then I can probably put up with it. Alice holds my hand as though she'll never let it go.

Waiting to go in to the grounds of The Manor House is a humiliating experience. I think so anyway. The gates are massive wrought-iron ones, barred like a tiger's cage at a zoo, only I'm not sure whether we're on the outside looking in or the inside looking out.

There's a large notice on a pillar at the side which says "NO beggars, NO hawkers and NO door-to-door salesmen."

I suppose, if anything, we must be in the category of beggars, so perhaps they won't let us in anyway. I'm not even sure what a hawker is unless it's person who keeps hawks but it seems a bit odd to be so specific about someone's taste in birds.

There's an intercom buzzer thing at the side of the gates too, which is just as well because the drive is so long you can't even see the house. It might take forever for someone to trail all the way down here to greet you, only to find you had a hawk about your person so you weren't allowed in after all.

Dad gazes through the bars with a look in his eyes the same as a child at a toyshop window. I wouldn't be surprised if he started drooling any minute.

"Oh Sal," he says, "One fine day we'll be living in a mansion exactly like this, just you wait."

Mum smiles and murmurs something kind in a half-hearted way so I know she's thinking "In your dreams,

Keith, you loser, and first it would be a help if you got off your backside and got yourself a job."

Dad, lost in the Land of Make-Believe, presses the buzzer and the intercom crackles into life. Through it comes an American woman's voice drawling, "Can't you read? No peasants." Then very quickly there's an awfully-awfully Englishman's voice saying, "Terribly sorry, strange sense of humour. Can I help you?"

And Dad says, "Hi Tristan, it's Keith."

And the toff's voice says, "Keith? Keith who?"

And I cringe. I expect Mum does too but I'm too busy cringing myself to notice anyone else's cringes.

"Why don't they just open the gate?" asks Alice, and Dad mutters, "I expect they're extremely busy."

There's a bit more crackling down the intercom and then the gates judder just once and begin to glide open without a sound.

"See, magic!" chirrups Dad, cheerful like a puppy again, only puppies don't chirrup. And Alice says, "That is not magic. That is modern technology. Probably Japanese."

I love Alice!

She still has hold of my hand and I give it a big squeeze and we begin the ten mile hike to the front door of The Manor House. Yes, I'm exaggerating again, but not much.

Half way there, already in need of refreshment, we are considerably cheered by the sight of Gloria (I'm assuming it's Gloria by a process of elimination because she doesn't look much like a Tristan) running towards us, bare-footed across the lawns wearing a floaty dress that's almost transparent and reaches her ankles.

I am cheered because her strange outfit makes Alice ask quite loudly, "Why is that woman wearing a nightie in the garden?" which causes Mum to squirm and go

"Sssssh!"

Dad is cheered by lascivious thoughts, if I am to believe anything that I've read about men. His mouth sags open anyway and Mum kicks him on the shin.

Gloria leaps over to us, her jibbly bits bouncing with every bound, so I'm sure Dad has to go to tremendous lengths to keep his jaw firmly in place. Then Gloria begins to gush at top volume, "Keith! Sally! How awwwwesome! And this must be daaaaahling little Alice…"

She doesn't mention me at all. It's as if I don't exist.

Chapter 40

Not existing, I discover, has its uses if you want to be an Undercover Reporter of Random Conversations. It's as though I have a Cloak of Invisibility all of my very own and people just carry on talking as if I'm not there. Either that or I'm as insignificant as a very small worm and not worthy of notice by anyone ever.

Anyway, at last, we are graciously admitted into The Manor House as long as we take our shoes off at the door, grovel profusely and tug our forelocks a lot (I made that up but it's what it feels like).

Tristan, the owner of The Manor House, and the awfully-awfully voice, is as pinkly plump as Gloria is tall and willowy. He wears very smart tweed hunting-shooting-fishing clothes similar to Bates the Gamekeeper, but a Bates the Gamekeeper who has been shopping at Harrods or some other posh place and never actually gone outside in his new outfit. Honestly, he looks like he hasn't hunted, shot or fished anything bigger than a tadpole in a jam jar.

At least Bates, horrible man though he is, Really Is Who He Really Is, not pretending to be Someone He's Not.

Dad is such a crawler I can't believe it, sucking up to a dipstick like Tristan. Has he no pride? Probably he'll melt into a slick of oil under the table if he doesn't stop being slimy very soon, but fortunately I don't have to witness it for long because the two of them ooze along to the study together to discuss Important Business or most probably drink vast amounts of alcohol even though it's only teatime.

That leaves me with The Girls. I don't know which is worse.

I am female. I have a female body. Female things

happen to it on a regular basis like once a month and it's a pain, however I do not feel the need to discuss all the gory little details with anyone else. What's in the slightest bit interesting about it? I'd have thought fully grown women would feel the same especially after so long putting up with it but I'm proved wrong with Mum and Gloria. It must be an age thing.

So here's *The Exciting Tale Of Gloria's Menstrual Cycle* as told to Mum in The Manor House kitchen while Alice sings to herself to block out the awfulness of it and I am apparently invisible. I bet you can't wait.

(Don't forget to read in a gushing American accent).

Here goes:

"Sally, honey, I can't begin to tell how Distraught I was, how Devastated! I was in pieces, Dahhhling, you can Imagine and I'm locked in the bathroom and Tristan taps relentlessly on the door simply begging for me to come out and discuss everything with him. Well, Sally, what is there to discuss? It's failed. There will be no baby. I just flushed the contents of my womb down the john for Chrissakes and Tristan is saying 'We can try again, Gloria, go back to the clinic,' but Sally, I'm through with clinics. 'There are other ways, Tristan,' I say, 'there are Other Ways,' and I'm about to tell him about The Sacred Ritual In The Woods and you'll never guess what he says, 'Gloria,' he says, 'What about adoption?' The retard! Why would I want someone else's little brat?"

And at that point she turns towards Alice, who's looking quite pale still singing madly in the corner of the kitchen and she says, "Come to Gloria, honeybunch. Gloria needs a hug from a pretty little girl."

In my opinion, Gloria doesn't need a hug so much as a slap.

Chapter 41

Gloria needs a slap and I need to get out of the kitchen before I die of revulsion or another fatal condition brought on by Too Much Gynaecological Information.

Wearing my non-existent cloak of invisibility, I follow the sound of drunken laughter to the study. I don't expect the men are talking about the workings of their private parts but check at the door to make sure because you can only take so much in one afternoon.

They are not, they are talking about golf. This is funny because Dad doesn't know anything about golf but I have noticed that if he has a few drinks he can talk about a lot of things he knows nothing about.

I slip in through the door and am greeted like a long lost relative but that's only due to the one and a half bottles of something with bubbles called Prosecco they have consumed.

Tristan is even pinker and Dad's already hiccupping and slurring his speech which is difficult to write but he says something to me like "Rosha, shweetiepie, would you like a glash of hic Proshecco to shoothe yer shavage hic breasht?"

No, I would *not* like a glass of Prosecco, thank you very much, if drinking it has the effect of turning me into a blabbering idiot. Aren't parents meant to be Positive Role Models or something?

Apart from Dad and Tristan's silliness ruining the atmosphere rather badly, the study is a place where I could happily spend years, days even.

There are floor-to-ceiling shelves and I've never seen so many books except in a library and those are only mostly Large Print Romances for old people so not what I call proper books. Perhaps Tristan isn't all bad, that's if he's actually read any of them and they're not just to make him seem intellectual, which he plainly isn't.

I choose a leather-bound volume which turns out to be *Alice Through the Looking Glass* and I wonder if it's A Sign then I curl up in a squashy old armchair and pretend to read. As a matter of fact, I *do* read but I also listen to Dad and Tristan's ramblings because I can do two things at once, or three if you count breathing as well.

"So, Kevin," says Tristan, and Dad doesn't bother to remind him his name's Keith or maybe Dad's so drunk he's forgotten his own name.

"So," says Tristan, "You're a fellow masochist with the old nine iron, are you?" (I think he's asking Dad if he enjoys golf).

Dad waves his arm vaguely in the air and says "Hole in one, old man!" Which is quite clever as ambiguous statements go.

Then Tristan unrolls a large piece of paper onto the table, weighing down the corners with Prosecco bottles and says to Dad, "Take a look at the plans for the golf complex, why don't you, Kevin? As I said before, I'd value your design input."

They both stand over the plans, Dad swaying slightly, making unintelligible comments until I completely lose interest and engross myself in Alice (the book not my sister).

That's until I hear something that makes me sit up and take notice...

"Of course," announces Tristan, "We'll need to bulldoze several acres of Wayland Woods, but no great loss to humanity, eh? The Wildings' cottage will have to go to begin with, not to mention that ridiculous place where the locals prance about semi-naked communing with Mother Nature or whatever it is they get up to in the dead of night trespassing on my property, the bastards."

Dad kind of blanches and gulps and takes a step backwards but Tristan doesn't seem to notice and goes on, "Yes, I have my gamekeeper hot on their heels, shotgun at the ready, but keep it under your hat, won't you old man?" he says, "We don't want any Revolting Peasants, now do we?"

Then he guffaws with laughter and so does Dad, but his laughter is to cover up the uncomfortable realisation that one of the Revolting Peasants is almost certainly his wife.

After that, Dad shuffles us all out of The Manor House pretty smartish.

Mum and Gloria cling to each other at the front door in a quite sickening way as though they've been friends for thirty years instead of thirty seconds and they haven't even been drinking.

Dad and Tristan do that sort of French kissing that men do, not the one with tongues down the throat.

I despair at my misfortune of being the child of two such mortifying parents.

"Bye-bye, Gloria," warbles Alice. "I hope your womb feels ever so much better soon."

If I had a brown paper bag, I'd stick it over my head.

Chapter 42

There are two main things running through my head as we make our way home that afternoon. One is that I should warn Caitlin about the destruction of Wayland Woods. The other is that I must escape from this place before I go insane.

Mixed up with the main things are zillions of lesser things that get in the way of my ability to make sensible plans.

These are:

1. I'm not speaking to Caitlin, so how can I warn her?
2. I don't think I should leave Alice behind
3. I don't want to take Alice with me because she's one of the things that's driving me insane
4. How much is a train ticket to London?

Okay, so that isn't zillions of things, but it's enough.

We get quite close to home and Dad announces he's off to the pub. I don't think Mum can have noticed the state he's in already, because all she does is kiss him on the cheek and says, "Think of your liver."

For a moment I wonder if that's what she had planned for his supper.

Normally I would try to stop Dad going to the pub For His Own Good but just at the moment I've got too much on my mind and my mind keeps changing every ten seconds.

"Warn Caitlin, she deserves it. Don't warn Caitlin, she's a bitch. Get away. Stay here. Take Alice. Leave Alice behind."

It's all too much.

I'd stay, definitely I would (or maybe I would) but keep remembering what Caitlin said about me and keep remembering the look of disgust on Kieron's face down by the river and know I simply can't bear to see either of them again.

It would be the worst form of humiliation.

So I make up my mind to go and decide to think about the other things later when my head has stopped threatening to explode.

If I had any doubts about leaving (which I did) they are quickly sent scurrying from the tangles of my brain by what happens next.

Chapter 43

When we get home, for some inexplicable reason Mum starts making bread. I'm wondering if she's pretending the dough is Dad by the way she's bashing it about on the kitchen table but perhaps it's only me who has these inventive ways of dealing with vicious feelings.

I am in the bedroom with Alice, making plans. Well, I am making plans and Alice is writing in her exercise book, one arm curved around it so I can't see what she's putting. She can't see what she's putting either but that doesn't seem to stop her writing.

I have just come up with the brilliant notion that I'll tell Mum and Dad I'm staying with Caitlin for a few days when I hear the kitchen door burst open and then the sound of raised voices. It doesn't sound like Dad back from the pub already so I think I should go downstairs in case it's a Mad Axe Murderer which is not an act of heroism to protect Mum, more of an act of curiosity. Alice hides under the blankets. This is an act of common sense quite unusual for someone who's a frootloop.

Now I recognize the other voice and it's *not* a Mad Axe Murderer unless he is one as well as being Caitlin's dad and I hadn't realised.

He's shouting, "You should've warned me. You should've, you stupid cow."

And Mum says, "Warned you? Warned you about what, Rhodri?"

I've just walked into the kitchen when he says, "You should've warned me that she's the spitting image of Deborah."

And they both stare at me, Caitlin's dad as though he's seen a ghost, Mum as though she's seen dog shit on the carpet.

"What are you saying about me and Auntie Deborah?" I ask, forgetting that I am not worthy of notice and so no-one answers me.

Instead, Mum slumps down onto a chair and says, "I didn't think."

Rhodri, (which is quicker to write than Caitlin's dad) snarls, inches from Mum's face, "No, you didn't think, did you? You didn't think then, and you didn't think now."

"I'm so sorry," says Mum in a tiny voice.

"So you said," growls Rhodri, "But it was too late by then, wasn't it, Sally?"

"Is anyone going to tell me what's going on?" I ask in an assertive way that couldn't have been very assertive at all because the only thing that happens is that Rhodri storms to the door and turns at the last second shouting, "God, I wish you'd never come back. I'm keeping well away from you. Both of you."

Then he looks at me again as though it pains his eyes and says with icy calm, "I don't take kindly to my kids being hurt by anyone. Anyone. Least of all the daughter of a...slag."

Then he's gone.

Didn't Caitlin say that her mother was a slag? The thought jumps into my brain that perhaps we're related and then jumps out again when I remember Caitlin's orange hair.

Mum gets to her feet once more and pounds the bread dough with all her might over and over and I think this time it could be Rhodri.

"Mum, will you tell me what's happening?" I ask.

She picks up that old photo of her and my auntie and rams it into a drawer. Then she says, "He's badly upset at the moment. His wife's not long left him because of the drinking. He doesn't know what he's saying. Please will you just go away, Rosa?"

Well, thank you, mother. Thank you very much. You just made up my mind for me.

Chapter 44

A bit later I slip out of the cottage with my back-pack stuffed full to bursting, unnoticed by Mum (which goes without saying) but with Alice tugging at my sleeve trying to stop me. I ignore her, keep walking, dragging her along behind me, but she won't let go.

"You don't have to leave," she says, tears sprouting out of the corners of her eyes like in a cartoon, which is hateful moral blackmail if you ask me.

"I *do* have to leave," I reply. "I can't bear this place any longer. I don't belong here and I'm going back to Notting Hill where people are normal."

"You really *really* don't have to go," says Alice, wrapping her arms around me, "Because soon, very soon…"

I don't give her the chance to finish whatever nonsense she's about to spout.

"Soon, very soon," I say, "When Kieron and Caitlin Wilding start talking, everyone in the whole of Wayland will know about me and my secret. Rosa The Weirdo. Let's all go to the freak show, have a good laugh."

"Not everyone's like that," she says.

I mutter I'd like to hear her name one and of course she does.

"Well, Megan wants to help you," she whispers.

I push her away now and yell at her, "You stay away from that old crone, do you hear me? You must promise me."

"No, I won't promise you," says Alice in a dignified way. "Megan is going to show me how to cure your face."

That stops me dead as though someone's tackled me from behind – but only for a millisecond before all the feelings come flooding back.

"There *is* no cure for my face at least not until I'm old enough for plastic surgery which is apparently when I've finished growing which is an adult's way of saying never."

"Megan's kind," says Alice. "She says she's going to take me to the altar in the woods and…"

At that moment, the giant hare leaps out of nowhere onto the path in front of us and makes a kind of hissing sound at Alice. I aim a kick at it and it glares at me, well, it *seems* to glare at me because of course hares don't glare, do they?

Do hares catch myxomatosis? I hope so because this animal is getting annoying.

"How *could* you?" says Alice, even though I'm sure I haven't said anything out loud. Then she flings her arms around me again and cries "Everything will be alright soon, you'll see. Then will you come home?"

"Of course I will," I lie. Then I tear myself from Alice's grasp and walk away from her without looking back.

If I look back I might not carry on.

Alice calls out to me, "Oh Rosa, I meant to tell you, Megan says you'll find Auntie Deborah in the churchyard."

Then I *do* look back but Alice has gone.

Chapter 45

My mind's a complete mess now. I won't even try to describe what a mess it's in because it's in such a mess that it's incapable of describing what a mess it's in.

My only thought is to get to the station but I know that's a lie as soon as I've written it. *One* of my thoughts is to get to the station. Other thoughts, demon thoughts, creep into my brain poking their long fingers and noses out of the shadows and very soon I find that my feet are taking me swiftly along the back lanes to the churchyard.

My feet have a lot to answer for.

By the time I get there the shadows are lengthening and churchyards are spooky places at the best of times but I have to admit that this churchyard has a peaceful feel to it, much more peaceful than my mind is at the moment.

The graves are all higgledy-piggledy ancient stone covered in moss and lichen and draped with tangly weeds so you can hardly read the inscriptions but it seems like they're loved somehow, still bathed in evening sunshine.

I know Auntie Deborah's not actually there in the churchyard. Not in real life. I mean, she's not going to pop out from behind a headstone saying, "Hi, I'm your dead auntie, the one who died long before you were born, the one who has the same birthmark as you." Is she?

I drift aimlessly around for a while wondering what I'm doing here when I should be on the station platform waiting for the next train to London, but there's something that keeps me there, a sort of Presence. Yes, I said A Presence and I don't even believe in stuff like that.

Presence or not, after a while, more and more a feeling creeps over me that I'm wasting my time and it's the moment to head for the gate... when something makes me look into the furthermost corner of the churchyard where I hadn't looked properly before.

It's so overgrown that there's nothing to be seen except brambles and a heap of grass cuttings and dead flowers. The churchyard rubbish tip.

Those feet of mine take me over there and I peer through the undergrowth and then, don't ask me how, but I know I've found her. I've found Auntie Deborah and it makes me want to cry.

In that labyrinth of twisty thorny branches there stands a solitary headstone with its back to me so I can't read what it might say on the front or who it might belong to, but I know.

I skirt round by the crumbling boundary wall and from the other side the bit in front of the grave is not so badly overgrown, though it's a bit like being that prince in *The Sleeping Beauty* thrashing my way through to it, scratched to ribbons but it doesn't seem important. The writing on the grave says:

DEBORAH ROSE GREENLAND
1960-1974

And a red patch the same shape as my birthmark bleeds across one half of the stone.

Chapter 46

She was only fourteen, my auntie, and she died and I don't know how she died and here she is in some abandoned corner of a graveyard by a rubbish tip all on her own and no-one talks about her and no-one takes care of her grave and she reminds me of *me* and it seems so unfair and I'm crying for her and crying for me and I'm tearing at the brambles all round her with my bare hands, just wanting to let a bit of light into her world, just wanting to set her free and then I hear a voice and stop.

Stop dead.

Dead as my Auntie Deborah. Only I'm still alive and fear is trembling in my lungs and galloping along my veins.

The voice is the voice I remember from that night at the altar in Wayland Woods, the voice of the King of The Freaky People and it's coming towards me and it's calling out and at first the words are indistinct but then they become creepily clear.

"I know you're in there, Rosa."

And I try not to breathe and peer out from amongst the brambles and I see him and it *is* The King of the Freaky People but this time he's not dressed in long white robes with a crown of oak leaves but in long black robes, only he does have a white collar round his neck and he is The Vicar.

I can remember gasping and then I must have fainted with the shock of it all because the next thing I know I'm lying out on the grass in the middle of the churchyard and can hear his voice praying over me but I don't open my eyes because I'm trying to shake off the disgusting thought that he's touched me and I don't know where, and it might only have been my ankles when he dragged me out of the bushes.

And he is praying in that voice you only hear in churches, "Look down from heaven Almighty God, we humbly beseech thee, with the eyes of mercy upon this child, now lying upon the bed of sickness…"

And I summon up every last ounce of my strength and scramble to my feet and grab my back-pack which, luckily for me is lying beside me, and I leg it out of the churchyard shouting, "Caitlin was right about you."

I only look back once and he's not following me, he's fallen to his knees and is doing some more praying, probably asking for forgiveness for being such a pervy creep.

Chapter 47

As I race along the lanes towards the station it's as though I'm attached to a bit of elastic and it's stretching and stretching as it tries to pull me back and the strands are fraying and might snap at any minute or it might just give up with the stretching and I'll find myself shooting backwards at high speed and crash landing at Auntie Deborah's graveside again.

In spite of all this, I know I have to get away even if it's not forever, because here too much keeps on happening, piling on top of me, drowning me in confusion so it's completely impossible to think straight.

Somehow the elastic stretches far enough for me to get to the station and I stop to catch my breath beside a green sign covered in flaky white writing which says UPPER WAYLAND HALT.

Even though it's late now, there's a light on in the crumbly old station building which could be straight out of a Thomas The Tank Engine book and, no, I don't still read them.

My hands are all bloody from the brambles and, not wanting to appear any more of a sight than I already do, I pull my sleeves right down over them and hope I won't need to fumble for change or anything.

Deep breath, shoulders back, look fearless Rosa, and I march into the station.

An elderly Station Master lurks in a glass-windowed ticket office drinking a cup of tea. I bend down to speak to him through the vent thing and have to take step backwards in surprise at the sight of his one mad, wandering eye. *Another* of those Wayland Woods freaks! He must be, because surely there can't be *two* people like that in one small village?

Quite honestly, so much surreal stuff keeps on happening that I'm pretty much past being surprised by anything. I step back to the vent and say in my best polite voice, "Excuse me, when is the next train to London?" which seems like an easy and reasonable question to me.

The Station Master rubs his chin and frowns.

"London, is it?" he ponders, as though I've inquired about a train to Outer Mongolia or Mars.

"Yes, London," I repeat, trying not to be impatient and he smiles and tells me I'm in luck, there's a train at nine thirty. My heart could burst with relief but then he adds, "Tomorrow morning."

I'm ready to start blubbing like a baby in a completely pathetic way I feel so exhausted by the strain of everything but then he says, very slowly, with lots of pauses, "But... there's another one... in twenty minutes."

I don't know whether I feel more like kicking him or hugging him and doing neither seems like the best option so I buy the ticket (One Way) with nearly all the money I possess in the whole wide world but hopefully Jules will lend me some when I get to her house.

I manage to sweep the change into my purse with my cuff so he doesn't even see my bloody hands which, by the way, are stinging like hell now.

"Will I need to change?" I ask which I suppose is a bit of a dumb question when I'm travelling from The Back Of Beyond all the way to London.

"Oh yes," he says in his snail's pace voice, "I think you will need to change a great deal." Then he pulls down the shutter of the ticket office.

CLACK.

It's lonely on the platform. Empty. Quiet as a grave, I think, and that makes me remember Auntie Deborah again so I stop thinking it.

I keep in the shadows, hoping no-one else will arrive, no-one like Mum for instance, alerted by that creep The Vicar or perhaps even Alice. I'm scared she might have blurted something out without meaning to. She's quite incapable of lying about anything when she's asked a direct question which is part of Her Condition.

At last, at last, the train trundles into view and I heave a huge sigh of something which might be relief or it might just be that I've been holding my breath for so long my body needs oxygen.

I shift my weary self towards the edge of the platform.

There's no-one else around but me.

The train hisses to a halt and I stand there like an idiot waiting for the door to slide open before realising I have to open it myself. With a door handle. How primitive. How very typical of this place.

I'm half way on board when a small hunched figure appears on the platform.

A small hunched figure that reminds me very much of Megan.

I don't mean she arrives, I mean one second she's not there and the next second she *is* there and my brain's gone into overdrive thinking I'll *never* escape from this place but she doesn't try to stop me. She just stares at me and I hear her voice though she isn't speaking and it says, "Leaving us so soon? I think not. Wayland would like you to stay. Wayland *requires* you to stay."

Then there's a cackle of laughter and the voice says, "Safe Journey, Rosa," and I slam the door behind me, the train starts up and rattles its way out of the station.

There's no-one on the platform when I look back.

Chapter 48

There's no-one in my carriage either. There's no-one in the rest of the train for all I know. Except for the driver. Presumably.

I sink down into a corner seat and wish it wasn't covered in that horrible scritchy-scratchy stuff because all I want to do is rest my head against it and go to sleep. But then I remember I have a whole back-pack full of clothes to use as a pillow and reach in and pull out a sweat-shirt. Bliss. Soft and scritch-free and smelling of me.

I snuggle up, close my eyes and listen to the jicketty-can jicketty-can jicketty-can of the train as it rattles its way slowly towards the first stop, a little town called Castle Cary. And then I know it will go on bigger and bigger places like Bath and Bristol and then I'll *really* be on the way back to The Biggest and Best Place of All, which is London.

I can't help wishing the train would go faster but at least it's going in the right direction.

Away.

About closing my eyes – The Good Bits
- It gives my eyelids a rest
- I don't have to look at the horrible patterned material covering the train seats
- It avoids the need for curtains when you're trying to sleep

About closing my eyes – The Bad Bits
- I see horrible things

Sometimes I see the girl's body under water tangled in weeds, and then the olden days girl running, running, her face transfixed with terror and the deformed baby squirming like an albino insect grub but mostly it's Alice I see, in glimpses and flashes that shift like a crazy kaleidoscope. She's an insect grub too, gross, alarming, all squishy body and, odder still, she has hare's ears. And now she's alone by the altar and tendrils of plants weave around her ankles and drag her into the ground and she's screaming "Rosa help me," and then she's in bed in a fever and tossing and turning and the beads of sweat on her brow get sucked back into her body and Megan has her round the throat with a clawed hand and…and…

So, I think the horrible patterned train seats might just be preferable and open my eyes.

And snap them shut again at once because sitting right opposite me is the very small man from the ritual, the one with the black and white streaky hair and he's so small his legs dangle off the edge of the seat, miles from the ground.

I can't decide if the sight of him is when my eyes are closed or when they're open so I experiment and he's definitely there in front of me and I shrink back into my seat and he stares and stares until I can't sit there any longer so get to my feet and just as I do that there's a screeching of the train brakes and a grinding, metal-shearing, spine-jolting

CRRRRRRRRUNCH

I'm thrown to the floor and, looking up, I can still see the little legs of The Very Small Man dangling off the edge of the seat and hear the sound of him laughing.

Chapter 49

If I had any breath left in my body I'd get up, but it has been knocked clean out of me so I'm just lying there my face on one side my nose almost stuck to a lump of chewing gum on the floor and there are half-eaten crisps and dust bunnies under the seats and if I was my Dad I'd be straight to my desk writing a letter of complaint to The Authorities telling them it Simply Isn't Good Enough.

The dangly legs have moved somewhere but I can still hear the laughing. Then the door between the carriages flies open and a man with polished black shoes and navy blue trousers stampedes up the aisle towards my face. I'm not sure what the rest of him is wearing. I can't see that far up.

You'd think he might have asked me if I was okay but he's too busy babbling like a lunatic, "It came out of nowhere, there wasn't a tree at all, then… there was a tree, a tree jumped onto the track straight in front of me."

Isn't that the sort of thing drunk drivers say when they hit a lamp-post? But in fairness, this man hasn't been drinking, as far as I know, and he does seem very upset, as you would be if a tree made a suicide bid in front of your train with no warning.

This must be The Driver, I think, with my remarkable powers of observation but I *have* just been in a train crash. He slumps down on a seat nearby moaning, head in hands and still The Very Small Man laughs on and on and on and squawks, "Après Nous Le Delusion," like a crazy parrot and even I in my befuddled state know that it should be Déluge not Delusion and it's French for We're Screwed, approximately, and I decide that if I don't get out of here very quickly I will be.

I seem to be doing a lot of struggling to my feet lately but here I go again, scooping up my sweat-shirt and my faithful back-pack and sprinting over to the train door. It's one of those where you have to open the window and reach down to the latch outside and I'm frantically groping for it.

The train driver finally manages to notice me and says, "Miss, we're in the middle of nowhere," and then his eyes glaze over and he murmurs "Nowhere... the tree came out of nowhere..."

I couldn't care less where we are as long as I'm not in the middle of a train carriage with a very small and sinister man and a babbling idiot so I wrench the door open at last and jump into the darkness.

Which is a Big Mistake.

The trackside is a bank of sharp and slidy stones that drops away into pitch blackness and there's me plunging downwards into who knows where, the sound of maniacal laughter reverberating in my ears and the agonizing feel of flesh ripping from my shins.

As I tumble, I'm sure Alice is below me tumbling even faster until she disappears, her hands stretched up trying to reach mine and that's not even with my eyes closed.

I come to rest in the bottom of a muddy ditch. Come to rest is a silly phrase that is a euphemism because it's a very misleading and kind way of describing the painful tangled heap in which I find myself and my assorted limbs, my back-pack and my sweat-shirt.

I'll hitch-hike to London instead, then.

Chapter 50

Yes, Mum's told me all the horror stories about hitch-hiking even though she did it herself when she was young (the hypocrite) but all this stuff has made me rash as German measles. Seriously loop-de-loopy.

I've-got-to-get-away-I've-got-to-get-away runs through my brain like a pop song that you hear on the radio and can't get out of your head for days and it drives me onwards when any sane person would have given up long ago and gone home.

Wherever that is.

Me scrambling to my feet is becoming as boring as my mouth dropping open in surprise but I'm sorry, it happens again.

I lurch out of the ditch, clamber up a grassy bank and drag myself over a wooden fence into a field. I can hear the train driver calling out, "Miss, Miss, are you injured?"

Now he's remembering his Passenger Care Awareness Training but it's too late for me.

Across the field there's the occasional flash of car headlights through distant trees as though it's a signal meant just for me, so that's where I head.

If I could get a lift to another place on the train route then I can still get to London. That's my plan, anyway, though if I were driving along in the dark doing no harm to anybody, I think I'd hesitate before picking *me* up with my bloody hands and my scraped shins, like an escaped convict without the leg shackles.

It's a bit of a slog to the road in the pale moonlight and all I can hear is my own breathing but it's better than hearing someone else's breathing. It's quite peaceful, otherwise, until an owl screeches and swoops across my line of vision just so I don't forget it's a spooky world out there.

Then there's a river. I wonder if it's *the* river. It could be. One river's very much like another river to me and someone please tell me why my life has turned into a Mega Obstacle Course all of a sudden. I'm just thinking I'll have to pretend to be a Boy Scout and fashion a bridge out of mud and bent twigs or whatever they do when I see that actually there *is* a bridge a bit further along. I cross it, counting my blessings, which doesn't take very long because I have so few.

After that it's only a very few steps to the road. It's not the widest of roads but it has traffic on it every so often which is the main thing.

It quickly occurs to me that I don't know which way to go, so therefore I don't know which verge to stand but, looking on the bright side even though it's dark, I can see vehicles in plenty of time and just nip across if necessary. The first car that stops I'll say, "I need to get to Bath, please," and the driver will either say 'Hop right in, girl!' or 'Are you losing your marbles? Bath is in the other direction."

I'll find out that way, easily enough.

That's the plan.

Best laid plans of mice and men and Rosa Cavanagh gang aft agley. Those last three strange words are ancient Scottish and mean Go Often Wrong and they are right because it *does* all go wrong.

Straightening out my tattered clothes as far as possible so I look less like The Creature From The Black Lagoon, I stand at the side of the road.

Waiting.

And waiting some more after the first bit of waiting.

Lots of time crawls by but no cars, then finally headlights approach and I step out boldly sticking my thumb out, full of optimism. The car speeds by without even hesitating.

And that happens again.
And again.
And my optimism is dwindling fast.

And then just when I think things can't get any worse they do. The sky is black velvet dotted with spangly stars and not a cloud to be seen anywhere and if I wasn't so desperate to get a lift I might have taken the time to appreciate how stunningly beautiful it is. But then it starts to rain. There's not only the rain falling in torrents but there's the boom of thunder and lightning forking all around me too and I'm drenched in no time flat even though I scurry for the shelter of the trees.

The weirdest thing about it all is that I can just about see through the rain ahead of me and it's not raining there. It's not raining behind me or on either side of me.

The only place it's raining is right on top of me and wherever I move it follows me as though there's a power shower attached to the sky directly above my head.

Yes, that's definitely weird. Or it's my mind playing tricks.

Chapter 51

I'm huddled under the trees now but it doesn't make any difference, the rain seeks me out which ever way I turn and it's cold and it's getting scary now, difficult to breathe properly with water streaming down my face, pouring into my mouth.

At my feet, water begins to rise up from the earth so I scramble to higher ground but the water rises further around me, my own tsunami wave threatening to sweep me away to oblivion. Could I outrun it? I don't know, I don't know anything at all anymore but it's the only thing that surfaces in my thoughts except to stay put and drown.

So I run.

And all the time I'm battling against the storm and the rising flood and the feeling that the world is trying to tell me something and I don't know what it is exactly but it's something to do with Alice being in danger and I must protect her.

I must not leave Wayland.

Faintly at first, getting stronger as I struggle towards it, I can see a light, the light of a lantern on the bank of the river.

In its glow, I can just make out an old white van and the figure of a man leaning against it, swigging from a flagon. Then he heaves a heavy box-shaped thing that looks like a car battery into the river and there's a SPLASH and a BOOM as loud as the thunder and with a huge net he starts scooping fish out of the water by the dozen, glinting silver in the moonlight.

And still I battle on towards him, already begging for his help but my voice is drowned out by the pounding of the rain.

He's bent over the water scooping fish and more

fish when, like a dam-burst, a tidal wave surges along the river, sweeping the net from his hands. With a roar of fury he stands up. Then in slow motion he turns towards me and I have never seen a face so terrified and it's the face of Rhodri, Caitlin's dad.

I'm screaming through the cascades of water, "Help me, please help me!" even though it's him, and he's backing away from me moaning, "No, no I didn't mean it Deborah," and he backs and he turns and bolts away SMACK into the clutches of Bates the Gamekeeper who roars "You bastard, Wilding!" and grabs him by the scruff of the neck.

Around me the rain stops as suddenly as it started, the water whooshes away and I fall to the ground exhausted.

And dry as a pile of laundry in the airing cupboard.

I can hear Rhodri whining, "Keep her off me, please keep her off me, I swear it was an accident."

The fearsome gruff voice of Bates snarls, "Cider talking, Wilding? You want to lay off that, you do. Lay off my bastard trout and all."

How did Bates not notice me?

I raise my head in time to see Rhodri being heaved away, his body dangling limply from Bates' grasp, like a puppet with its strings cut.

Nearby, half concealed in the trees, there's a Land Rover and Bates bundles Rhodri into the back shouting, "It's the lock-up for you, you thieving poaching scumbag."

Then the engine starts and the Land Rover bounces off across the fields.

How I get back to Wayland village I don't know but I manage it somehow and the only friendly place I can think of for the moment is Auntie Deborah's grave and, curled up next to her, one arm wrapped around the headstone, I fall into a fitful sleep until the morning.

Chapter 52

I wake with dappled sunshine playing on my face, strangely rested as though I've spent the night in a soft feather bed not in a makeshift nest amongst the brambles by an abandoned grave or, I should say, a grave that *was* abandoned until yesterday but won't ever be again.

I crouch next to it watching water trickle down one side of the headstone like tears and with one forefinger I trace the words of the inscription.

Deborah Rose.

They always told me I was named after Rosa Parks, that black woman in Alabama who refused to give up her seat on the bus, but it seems that was a lie too. I'm quickly coming to the conclusion that my entire family history is constructed of lies and omissions and it's not just the history it's the *now* and I'm going to get it straight once and for all, before the feeling of dread in the pit of my stomach becomes more than a feeling and turns into a horrible reality.

I make my way slowly back to the cottage, warmed by the gentle morning sunshine, and creep up the stairs to our bedroom, holding my breath in case I'm too late and Alice isn't there.

My fears are unfounded, at least for the moment. (A very short moment). She's cuddled up in bed, a drowsy smile on her lips, and she whispers, "I knew you'd come back."

"I didn't know I'd come back," I say.

"Hail redemption's happy dawn," she murmurs.

And then I notice she has hare's ears and I shudder and rip back the blankets. She blinks, startled. She's wrapped up tight as...tight as an insect grub, limbless and revolting.

This is it. My nightmare. My nightmare's following me like a shadow. Everything's so tangled in my mind and I groan, cover my eyes with my hands and bend double, cramped to the very pit of my soul.

"Do you like it?" says Alice.

Do I like it? Do I like seeing a hideous vision come to life in front of my eyes? I don't think so.

"Megan gave it to me. It's my favourite. Except it's difficult to go to the loo," she beams.

Megan.

No.

Enough.

Everything sags. My expression, my weary legs, my thought processes, everything. I manage to stagger to my bed and nose-dive into the dubious comfort of the blankets.

"The weirdest things keep happening, Alice. Have you any idea what's going on?"

Before she has time to answer, if she was going to answer at all, there's the sound of Dad's clumping footsteps outside the room and he's singing, "Good morning, good morning, we've danced the whole night through, good morning, good morning to you!"

"What's going on," Alice says, "is that Daddy got out of bed on the right side for a change."

Well, I think that's what she said, but I was drifting off to sleep at the time.

Chapter 53

There are loads of expressions I've read in some book somewhere like 'Strike While The Iron's Hot!' and 'Grasp The Nettle!' and 'No More Beating About The Bush!' and others that escape me for the moment.

I decide to do them all simultaneously as soon as I wake up again.

Alice is singing in the bath and I wouldn't be surprised if a whale didn't force its way up the plughole in the very near future because if you've ever heard a whale song that's exactly what she sounds like. At least it's slightly more bearable than her cat-strangling repertoire.

The hare-grub costume lies crumpled on top of her bed like a mutated skin, empty of life, and I ram it under the pillow so I won't have to look at it.

I make myself look presentable, which is to say presentable to *me,* with make-up on my face and clothes that would make your granny shudder. The scratches on my hands and the scrapes on my shin aren't there anymore and I go into one of those foolish states of thinking, "Well maybe I imagined it? Maybe I imagined *everything*?"

But I'm sure I didn't.

I stride down the stairs and into the kitchen where Mum sits at the table making a sort of elvish garland out of twisted foliage and flowers. She would make a very good scarecrow if you stood her in a field with a broom handle shoved up the back of her dress.

I'm certain she flinches when I appear and she flinches even more when I start talking to her. She's not used to me communicating very much so it must come as something of a shock.

She's prattling on about anything and nothing at all just to keep my questions at bay but I say, very sternly, "Mum!" and she stops with a rabbit-in-the-headlights face.

I want to know about Auntie Deborah, I say.

BAM!

"Deborah? What have they been saying? They have no right, no right at all," she gibbers and her hands shake so much she drops the garland on the floor.

My puzzled expression makes her go on gibbering. "The Wildings. What have they been saying? Don't believe it, whatever it is."

"What are you talking about, mother?" I say, with unusual glacial calm.

She gets up from the table and, head bowed, goes to the dresser and opens the drawer, the drawer where she shoved that photo. It's still there. She brings it back to the table and smoothes its crumpled edges with the palm of her hand though she can hardly bear to look at it.

"Why do you and Dad never mention her?" I say, more gently.

She runs a finger down the side of Auntie Deborah's face.

"It was a long time ago," she whispers, as if that's a good enough explanation.

"How did she die?" I think I know already. I just want her to *say it*. She can hardly get the words out.

"She drowned."

"In the river?" I ask. She nods and I say, "I saw."

I might as well have shot her with a Taser gun. She rockets from the chair mumbling, "Don't be so ridiculous. What are you saying, you saw?"

"I saw a girl's body tangled in the reeds. Just for a second."

Mum's crying now, "You thought, you *thought* you saw."

And then she runs from the room.

"I know what I saw," I shout after her, and I just catch her muttering, "You always did have a fertile imagination, Rosa."

Then the door slams.

Well, that was an outstanding success, wasn't it?

Chapter 54

Alice is still in the bath when I go upstairs but she's no longer communing with whales.

"I'm off out," I shout through the door.

"Don't be late, will you?" she shouts back, although Alice never really shouts, it's more of a loud twitter.

Late for what? What's she going on about? Alice answers my question before I even ask it. "*You* know, Rosa," she says, "The Special Expedition, where we get ready for The Mystic Circle of the Young Girl."

Uh?

"It's all to do with Gloria's womb and your face," she finishes, then starts singing again.

I say "Good grief," more to myself than to her and decide that I *certainly* better not be late back.

The reason I'm off out, by the way, is that I'm going to visit Deborah and tidy her grave. I'm not calling her Auntie Deborah anymore because she's the same age as me and she was never really my auntie, when you come to think about it,

I expect you're concluding that I'm a sad person, a Billy-No-Mates, a pitiful and weird person, when my best and only friend is a Dead Person. Not just any old Dead Person but My Dead Aunt.

I'd just like you to know that I don't need any other friends.

Chapter 55

In the garden, Dad doesn't notice me as I make my way to the gate with a pair of those garden scissor things (secateurs, I think they're called) in one hand.

He's digging furiously, tossing mangled vegetation into a wheelbarrow. He's got unsightly sweaty patches on his shirt and I hope no-one important comes round because it's quite disgusting. I stop for a minute to watch this unaccustomed burst of activity from a man who rarely moves his backside from a chair.

He digs a patch, then, as soon as he's moved on to the next bit, the plants appear to grow back again, shooting up out of the earth as though they're on springs. Either that or he Hasn't Done A Thorough Enough Job, which is what he's always accusing me of. Whatever the case it's funny.

With a roar he throws down his spade, bellowing to the skies, "A vegetable garden she wants! A spade-diggin' sweat-makin' back-breakin' ball-numbin' vegetable garden. I'm an artist! Doesn't she understand? Perhaps she could effing well…"

Then he does notice me giggling in the background and makes a sort of humphing sound.

"Bye, Daddy," I say sweetly and skip off before he clips me round the ear hole. He wouldn't *really* do that because it's against the law but he quite often pretends to do it in moments of anguish and one day his hand might slip.

The heat of the day is so intense by now that the air thrums and shimmers along the hedgerows and the smell of blossom is sweet in my nostrils but on the downside the drone of insects could get annoying. There's not a soul out and about on the lanes as I walk along to the church and that pleases me because I don't want to meet any souls.

I want time to think, to put the muddled and dark thoughts into some sort of order. I wish I'd thought to bring a pencil and a notebook so I could make a list. A very long list. Or I could draw a mind-map. But that could be scary with the state of my mind at the moment when it's not distracted by comical scenes starring My Idiotic Dad.

As I get nearer to the church, the noise of the insects is drowned out by another louder noise, the insistent whiny buzz of a grass mower.

It looks as though my planned time of peaceful contemplation is going to be ruined, particularly as the man who's pushing the machine between the graves has dreadlocks tumbling right down his back and, if by any chance anyone needs reminding, he's one of the Freaky People. *Another* one of the Freaky People. They're everywhere.

Still, I'm feeling calm and bold, if it's possible to feel both of those things at the same time, and on top of that I have a sudden burst of inspiration, which doesn't happen that often. I'll ask him to mow round Deborah's grave and that'll save my arms from the worst of the brambles.

I shout over the noise of the mower until he turns it off and I point towards Deborah's corner, my mouth half open ready to make the request, but Deborah's corner has already been mowed. In fact, that *can't* be Deborah's corner because there is no headstone there. I spin wildly to check out the other corners all the time knowing it was *that* corner, it definitely, definitely *was* that corner.

The Dreadlock Man gazes at me oddly but I expect he has good reason. I've never stammered before but I do then, which looks messy on the page when you write it, "Th-th-the headstone th-th-that was in th-th-that corner..?"

"There's never been a headstone in that corner," he interrupts, arms folded across his chest, before I can stammer any more.

But there was. I *know* there was. I race over there and examine the ground. There's an oblong patch of darker grass and the earth seems to move under it in hardly visible waves.

"Look!" I shriek and then I think Mum's peering over the wall but she's gone before I open my mouth to shout out to her and The Vicar is at my side all of a sudden, as well as The Dreadlock Man and I cringe and he asks what we're meant to be looking at, his voice filled with disdain.

I'm about to tell him, panic creeping up my throat, but something inside warns me not to. He puts his bony hand out towards my brow, I suppose to feel for fever and I'm screaming, "Don't touch me!" At the same moment, he's saying, "Maybe the heat is making her hallucinate?"

They both loom over me casting their shadows on my body, pretending to be concerned but I know they're not. I'm shouting, "No, no, it's not me, it's really happening. No-one sees anything but me, no-one but me and Alice."

The two men exchange glances.

"Ah, Alice!" says The Dreadlock Man. "Alice The Chosen One."

Chapter 56

I think I'm going to be sick. All these strange things happen to me and then everything goes quiet for a while and I'm lulled into a false sense of security, thinking that nothing is as bad as it seems and it'll only take a little resourcefulness on my part to sort it out and then WHAM another thing happens.

My life at the moment is all about running away. Running away from weird things, running away from freaky people and malevolent old women, running away from unfriendly places and most likely running away from myself too, but that's a bit deep and psychological. It's about time I stopped. I don't mean stop running, but stop running *away,* so as I sprint out of the churchyard, let me inform you I'm not running away from The Vicar and The Dreadlock Man, I am running *towards* Alice. And that paragraph has running in it eight times, or nine if you count the last one, which must be something of a record.

I am running towards Alice because I fear the worst and must warn her and protect her, added to which, it's almost time for the expedition.

The Mystic Circle Of The Young Girl? To me that phrase is beginning to sound more and more sick as each minute goes by. Worrying thoughts of virgin sacrifices creep up on me out of nowhere. It must be out of nowhere because I can truthfully say I've never thought about them before.

I'm so busy trying not to think about virgin sacrifices as I hurry along the lane that the old white van is almost upon me before I notice it and I have to fling myself out of its erratic path into the hedge.

That white van. The one by the river last night. Rhodri's white van. Now he's trying to kill me. Or he's been at the cider again. (No wonder his wife left him).

The van slews diagonally across the road, and the engine, which sounds like a Jumbo Jet with laryngitis, cuts out with a throaty whimper.

I'm just trying to gather my shattered nerves together to make my escape (and you can forget all those fine sentiments about not running away anymore) when the driver's door squeaks open on its rusty hinges and out steps...

Caitlin.

Caitlin. Top of the list of people I don't want to see. (Second top, at least, immediately below Kieron) The power of speech deserts me. Thanks, power of speech. She's fourteen years old and she's just tried to finish me off using her dad's van as A Lethal Weapon and no suitable words are to be found in the recesses of my traumatised brain.

"You can run but you can't hide," she says.

I'm not hiding but I am sprawled in the hedge, not exactly in a position to defend myself adequately.

"So I was a cow," I say, "but that's no reason to mow me down in your dad's van."

"I wasn't mowing you down," she says. "I was trying to steer. And yes, you were a cow. Queen Cow of Cowland, actually."

I mutter that I'm sorry, in a voice that's quiet enough so she doesn't hear it because I don't want to show any weakness. She has that defiant, cocky look on her face the same as the first day at school but perhaps it's some sort of mask because it suddenly dissolves into worry and she tells me she's lost her dad.

"How careless!" I snap, pulling myself upright and removing twigs from my hair, then immediately regret being a smartypants when her eyes fill with tears and she says, "Get stuffed, Rosa," and climbs back into the van.

This time I mutter "I'm sorry" a tiny bit louder but her only response, through the wound-down window, is "Yeah right, of course you are."

Which I think I probably deserve.

"I saw him last night," I say, to make amends, and she asks, "How come?"

So I tell her all about what happened, not including the personal rainstorm bit because that's too weird, and she calls me a nutty tart for even thinking of asking her dad for a lift. She's brightened up a bit by now and she says, "Well, at least he's not face down in the river!"

What is it with people in rivers round here?

"Anyway, where were you off to in such a screaming hurry?" she asks, quite back to the cheerful Caitlin I used to be friends with yesterday, which makes me cheerful too. (Dead aunts really aren't the best company, if I'm honest).

"Actually, I was trying to find Alice," I confess to her a little reluctantly. I wish I hadn't.

"Oh, the Alice that you don't give a monkey's about? The Alice that if you never saw her smarmy little face ever again it'd be too soon?" she smirks.

"Yep, *that* Alice."

"Well hop in then," she says. "I'll give you a lift."

"Like I want to die?"

"Like you can walk if you're that bothered," she says.

137

Chapter 57

Being driven by Caitlin isn't too bad as long as you have your hands over your eyes. I wish for another pair of hands, though, because it would be good to have some extra extremities to clutch on to the dashboard. Isn't what we're doing meant to be called joy-riding? Believe me it's not in the slightest bit joyful. Stomach-churningly, bottom-clenchingly scary, yes.

"Where are we going?" she inquires cheerily, as the van kangaroo hops round a double-bend.

I peep through my fingers momentarily. "The right side of the road would be good."

To distract me from the fear of a plunge into the nearest ditch or a head-on collision with a suicidal tree I tell her about The Vicar and The Dreadlock Man. She isn't impressed.

"You're losing it, you are, Rosa. What are you talking about, Alice, the Chosen One?"

"There's something going on, I say," which seems a bit surplus to requirements as statements go, after what's been happening in the last few days.

"All that stuff in the woods, it's just kiddies' playtime for grown-ups," she says. And *then* she says, "Oh yeah, and if you're wondering where your boot is, Kieron's got it."

Why do faces have to do things like go pink? At least it's under the make-up but you could toast marshmallows on my cheeks.

"He found it in the river when we were looking for Dad," she goes on, loving every minute of me squirming in my seat. The bitch.

Then she gives me a sly sideways glance and says "He's probably put it under his pillow. Or he's sniffing it."

"Why would he want to do that?" I mutter under my breath.

"Duh!" says Caitlin and I tell her to drop dead. Then she stamps on the brakes and we kerthump into the verge right outside the cottage and I just about avoid going head first through the windscreen.

"Thank you so much, I'll walk next time," I say as I crawl out of the van on jelly legs.

She gives me the finger and begins a ten-point turn on the pavement. And nearly my toes. Then she sets off on her bouncing way to look for her dad.

And then I remember I forgot to warn her about the plans to demolish her home.

Chapter 58

Back to Alice. Quickly. Before I'm forced to think about Kieron.

She's at the kitchen table when I go inside, drawing in her exercise book. Without looking up she says, "Megan saw you in the churchyard. She told me. What were you doing there?"

I feel sick again. Sick with the thought that Megan must have been following me, watching me, and I didn't even know it and even more sick with the thought that Megan has been here with Alice again.

"Alice, please keep away from Megan," I say.

"Why would she want to do that?" croaks Megan, appearing in the doorway, making me jump half out of my skin. No, more like three quarters.

"Yes, why would she want to do that?" says Mum, right behind her.

"Yes, why would I want to do that?" says Alice, smiling sweetly up at me.

Do you ever get the feeling that you're *outnumbered*? I stutter and mutter a bit but no-one's interested. They have their minds on other things.

"Right," says Mum briskly, "are you ready, Alice?"

"When the will is ready, the feet are light," she chirps in that annoying little way of hers, making me forget just for a moment that I've made my mind up never to be annoyed by her ever again.

"Bye-bye, Mummy, Bye-bye Rosa," she warbles and skips over to Megan, taking a clawed old hand in hers. Megan licks her lips. (*Her* lips not Alice's. Gross thought).

Wait a minute, what does Alice mean 'bye-bye'?

"Aren't you going with them, Mum?" I ask, and she says, "Why? They're only going for a walk, Rosa."

"A very *special* walk," says Alice, and Megan's

eyes narrow, if I'm not much mistaken.

"Well, I'm coming too," I say.

There are three different reactions to this.

1. Alice says "Goody goody gumdrops!"
2. Mum says "But you don't *like* going for walks, Rosa."
3. Megan hisses

"I've made up my mind," I announce.

Megan's eyes are now so narrow that they're almost invisible slits. She pulls Alice quite roughly towards the door.

I follow.

Alice's exercise book is lying open on the table. There's a picture of some woods and there's that medieval girl running through them. Really running. I mean *moving* across the page. I make a strangled gulping sound and the girl disappears.

Mum and Alice look at me oddly, Alice with her head tilted to one side speculatively, and Megan smiles at me. Usually when you say someone smiles at you, it's a *nice* thing to report, but Megan's smile isn't a friendly smile. I am sure it has evil behind it, that's unless I'm completely losing my marbles.

Maybe I am.

I glance down at the page again to check on the state of my marbles and words appear right over the picture. Oh dear about my marbles. I blink but the words don't go away. The words say:

WAYLAND WOODS
PRIVATE PROPERTY
TRESPASSERS WILL BE PROSECUTED

"How do you do that, Alice?" I ask.

"Do what?" she and Mum ask in the same breath.

And Megan pulls Alice out through the back door.

Chapter 59

I now know what it's like to be a gooseberry. Not a little hairy green fruit that you make into jam or put into pies, but someone who is not welcome in the company of two other people. Actually, I think Alice likes me being there but Megan's displeasure comes off her scrawny hunched-up old body in waves.

We must make an odd sight, the three of us, Alice holding my hand on one side and Megan's on the other, skipping along beside the woods happily chatting, and me and Megan glowering at one another over her head. I'm simply *not* going to let go of my sister. Not for a single second.

Just when you think things couldn't get any more uncomfortable they do. Ahead of us on the track is Bates the Gamekeeper with a huge sledgehammer, knocking a wooden post into the ground. The THUD THUD THUD makes my ears twang. Inside, I mean.

At a safe distance stands Tristan, arms folded, Lord Muck of The Manor watching the servant at work and doing none himself. At least if he's there, Bates might not use the sledgehammer on *us*.

"Out for a stroll, ladies?" asks Tristan in his piggy upper-class voice as we draw level with him.

He's bright, isn't he? It must have taken great intelligence to work that one out and I'm just about to make a sarcastic comment when Alice pipes up "Yes we *are*! We're just going to the...OUCH."

The OUCH is where Megan has kicked her on the ankle to shut her up.

"We're just going across the fields," Megan says quickly and firmly, and before Alice has a chance to be truthful we yank her a bit further along the track.

Bates is nailing a sign to the post and my heart

jumps into my mouth because it says, in exactly the same writing as in the exercise book:

WAYLAND WOODS
PRIVATE PROPERTY
TRESPASSERS WILL BE PROSECUTED

This would be one of those moments where my mouth drops open in surprise (even if it already has my heart in it) if I hadn't given up doing that. I think it drops open anyway.

Tristan comes up behind us and speaks to Bates as though we aren't there. I suppose he does that quite a lot in the company of peasants.

"That's told 'em, eh, Bates?" he says.

"Them as can read, anywaysup," says Bates, leering at us in a very rude way. I think my mouth is still jammed in the open position so I don't respond and neither does Alice for once. Megan does one of her hisses which is quite fitting for a change.

Bates and Tristan trudge off.

As they do, the words on the sign fade into nothingness.

"So are we allowed in the woods or not?" asks Alice, while I'm busy rubbing my eyes in disbelief though why people do that and expect it to make a difference is anyone's guess and it doesn't because the words are still gone.

"Oh yes," replies Megan, "Yes indeed we are allowed. No earthly man can claim ownership of Wayland Woods."

Chapter 60

Wayland Woods seem to want to claim ownership of *us* though. It's quite a strangling suffocating feeling as we force our way through its clutches towards the altar. Trees press in closely all around us, branches catch at our clothes and thorns do their prickly best to scratch our faces.

It was broad daylight when we left the track but now there are only occasional glimpses of sunlight through the highest branches of the trees, otherwise it's as dark as black and leaves rustle in a breeze that has blown in out of nowhere and they seem to be whispering Alice's name. Aaaaalisss, Aaaaalisssssss, Aaaaalisssssssssss. Or is that what rustling leaves *always* sound like? I don't know.

Megan is in front, wizened hand clutching one of Alice's, dragging her along. It's impossible for me to hold her other hand any more. It takes all my strength to keep close behind her. It's as though the trees are trying to force us further and further apart.

Alice turns to me, her face paper white in the gloom and she says, "I don't like it here, Rosa."

At the same moment, Megan looks round too. Her eyes flash brightly and BLAM! we're in a clearing bathed in sunlight.

And suddenly it's as though we're all out for a jolly picnic only there are no sandwiches. Well, no picnic at all, actually.

Alice, Megan and I sit on a mossy bank in a row chatting like ordinary people chat about the weather and the wild flowers and the merry hum of the little buzzy bees and I kind of laugh inside because I used to find this sort of thing so tedious but I quite like the countryside now. I haven't thought about Notting Hill for *hours* and when I do it's all bustle and dirt and noise in my mind and not that appealing anymore. To think I wanted to run away from here to there...

Caitlin's words run around in my head – the words that said all the stuff in the woods is just kiddies' playtime for grown-ups. Perhaps it is. And if it *is* then the creeping realisation comes upon me that I am going mad. And a second creeping realisation comes upon me that I'm sure I'm *not* going mad (what about all the Deborah stuff, for instance?) And then a third creeping realisation comes upon me that if I *am* going mad I'm bound to have all these creeping realisations and it will be impossible to decide which ones to trust.

Why does life have to be so difficult?

While I'm occupied with all these significant thoughts, Alice is bouncing up and down on the mossy bank begging and pleading with Megan to tell us a story as though we're little children at bedtime waiting for the next instalment of *Peter Rabbit*.

"Very well," Megan says, and a shadow passes over the mossy bank.

"Indeed, it is a legend shrouded in the mists of time," she begins.

"And Rosa still bears the scar," announces Alice gleefully.

The jolly picnic moment evaporates into dark oblivion. "What is this?" I scowl.

"It's your story, Rosa! Megan's been telling me and I've been writing it down. It's called *The Curse of the First Born Girls*."

WHAT?

"Well, thank you very much, little sister. I don't want to hear one word of this load of made-up horse excrement but if it makes you happy..." (It's just the last five words of that sentence that actually come out of my mouth which only goes to show how weasly and pathetic I really am).

So.

Here is what I heard, in Megan's treacly voice - up until the bit where I fall asleep.

It befell in the days of Uther Pendragon, there was a gentle damosel, Elinor, full young and tender of age. She was but fourteen winters old, a garland of flowers ever about her head. And many were there desired her and many she turned away. Her heart it belonged to Aodhán, a full likely man well made of body. He looked upon her fair face and his heart was hers. And so they burnt both in love and the touch of her hand ever liveth in his skin.

And thus they passed together many a long day of contentment until came the season of harvest moon. Ano, Aodhán asked of his maiden to walk awhile into Wayland Woods there to take pleasure. And right as she promised she came.

Deep into the wood and deeper still they wandered thinking not of the way. Through the perilous passages they went knowing not of the passing of the hours and hearing not the trees calling them ever onwards into places hidden from the eyes of men...

And it's about here I doze off. The words are so beautiful, Megan's voice so soothing, so *hypnotic* that my eyes are getting sleepy, sleepy, and when I'm asleep all the bits of my dreams with the medieval girl, who must surely be Elinor, fall into place like the pieces of a jigsaw – the stealing of a pretty little baby in the woods and running away in fear, the baby changing into a horrible squalling creature with a blemish and Elinor looking into the water and her face becomes stained and...

Alice is right or at least not entirely wrong. The

story could almost be about me in another faraway realm. Almost. Almost.

Yes, the words are so *hypnotic*...

And then I wake up to find that Alice and Megan have gone.

Chapter 61

It was a *trick* wasn't it? A ghastly, devious trick.

Megan hypnotised me so she could get her hands on Alice. I'm *not* going mad, *am* I? (I'm afraid you only have my word for it at the moment).

The altar. I must get to the altar. If only I'd concentrated at Brownies when we did that tracking badge thing. Living in Notting Hill it seemed a bit of a waste of time learning about animal footprints and broken twigs and so on. Do they even *have* broken twigs in Notting Hill? I doubt it.

I look around wildly, wondering which path to follow. This is another futile exercise because there aren't any paths anyway, just entwined trees preventing me from going anywhere at all.

Then, from very far away, I hear a terrible scream. It sounds like a terrible scream from a distance so imagine what it must have sounded like if you were right next to it.

And I scream too but it's not a terrible one. I don't *do* terrible screams. Instead I scream "Alice!" which reverberates round the woods as though I've screamed it twenty times.

I'm sure following the sounds of distant screams didn't feature in the Brownies but perhaps they should consider it. So here I am again bashing and crashing my way through trees and shrubs and undergrowth like a mad thing and thinking how useful a machete would be and do they sell them in B&Q?

There are no more distant screams to guide me but there are instead some less distant moaning and groaning sounds so I know I must be getting close. Close to what, though? I hardly dare to think about it.

Then, ahead of me through the tangled knots of the

undergrowth, I see them. Alice and Megan. Alice and Megan hurrying hand in hand along a perfectly clear path which means I've been putting myself through all this foliage-related torture for nothing.

Everything seems to be quite normal. Alice certainly doesn't look as though she's being dragged somewhere against her will. Unless...unless of course *she's* been hypnotised as well.

My first thought is to charge after them and rescue Alice with Great Bravado but

a) She may not *need* rescuing and then I would look like a complete idiot
b) If I creep up behind them it might be possible to find out if there *is* a devious plot or if it's all completely innocent.
c) Great Bravado has disappeared somewhere without telling me

So I creep.

And a pretty good job I do of it, if I say so myself.

The woodland is vaguely familiar now and I realise we're very close to the altar. My realisation is helped by the fact that there are strange wailings in the air and it sounds very much like Gloria doing something odd.

I'm almost up to Megan and Alice and they're nearly at the clearing when Megan stops dead and pushes Alice behind her, hissing, "Curse you!"

I was right about Gloria.

She's dressed in white robes, busy setting fire to dried leaves on the altar, scattering strange powders into the flames which fizz and pop like little fireworks. She inhales a great noseful of the smoke then has a bit of a cough and a splutter, which I'm sure wasn't part of the ritual.

She rends the air with a wail of "Oh most blessed

Mother Goddess, show me I am liken unto the ripest of all fruit that I may bear a child," then she prostrates herself, in serious danger of setting fire to her hair, if you ask me.

Her final, piercing cry is, "My womb overflows with the power of night and light!"

Then she collapses.

Get a grip, Gloria!

"Is she okay?" whispers Alice to Megan.

"She is a hindrance," snaps Megan," the time grows ever closer…"

Alice has just said, "You mean, the time when I can heal Rosa?" and I lean forward to hear better, tread on a branch by accident, there's a loud

CRACK

and Megan and Alice spin round.

"We thought you were asleep," says Alice. "You looked so peaceful lying there."

Megan's hands clench in fury and she says nothing.

Chapter 62

Gloria lies exhausted on the altar, so exhausted that she doesn't seem to be aware of our presence. Either that or she's too embarrassed to open her eyes after making such an exhibition of herself.

Megan strokes her brow, soothes her with kind words. So much for thinking she's a hindrance.

"It's time you and I set off for home, don't you think, Alice?" I say pointedly.

Megan bristles with indignation. "There's really no need. No need at all. Is there Alice?"

"No need at all," says Alice. (I can always rely on Alice to support me in times of need).

Gloria props herself up on one elbow. "Alice?" she murmurs weakly. "Alice The Chosen One?"

"Alice Cavanagh, actually," says Alice primly. (I can always rely on Alice to make me smile about ten seconds after she's made me scowl with fury about something else).

"Stay safe for me, little girl," whispers Gloria. "See you tomorrow."

"What's happening tomorrow?" I ask. It's very difficult to keep up with everything sometimes and it always seems to be me who's the last one to know anything.

"The Preparation For The Ritual," says Alice. "Isn't it exciting?"

Megan runs the tip of her tongue round her lips and Gloria swoons again. The Preparation For The Ritual is *that* exciting? I don't like the sound of it. I don't like the sound of it *at all*.

"We're off now," I say firmly and haul Alice away from the altar amidst all her squeaky protestations, Megan's disapproving mutters and Gloria's mournful wails. Imagine the noises you'd hear during feeding time at a monkey house and that would be about right and I'm wondering if I'm the only sane person in the entire universe until remembering I might be going mad.

Chapter 63

Looking back over the last few pages, it mentions Alice and Megan hurrying hand in hand along a perfectly clear path. I wrote that because that's what was *there.* There was a perfectly clear path. And now it's gone. And before you wonder about my sense of direction, it *is* the same path or rather it's the same path that is no longer a path because you can't go down it anymore, so path is the wrong name for it.

All around us leaves flutter and spin to the ground and leaves shouldn't fall from trees when they're green, should they? Not even in autumn. Little woodland animals, rabbits, foxes, mice scurry ahead of us, birds shriek out alarm calls. Wayland Woods is alive with danger.

I know it's something to do with Alice. And something, I have no idea what, tracks Alice's every move from the trees. Or maybe it's the trees themselves?

I'm not part of the plan, whatever that plan is. I'm not touched. With my every step, a path opens up in front of me as though the woods can't wait to hurry me along and spit me out at the other end, but with Alice...

The trees creak and moan, bending over her like a living cage trap. Branches furl and weave around her body like snakes and I beat them off with my bare hands and wish I was wearing gloves.

Alice wanders along oblivious to the turmoil that surrounds her, singing in her strange, ethereal voice. It seems like hours but it can only be a matter of minutes before we're out of the woods into the sunlight but still they won't let her go, still she's in some sort of dream existence as though her mind has been spirited away and it's only a matter of time before her body follows.

Her hair and dress are drawn out sideways as though she's being sucked back into Wayland Woods from the track, gently at first then with more force. She has to battle to keep walking in a straight line and I cling onto her hand with all my might trying to get her home, to safety, to anywhere but here. Soon it's a struggle to keep her upright. Some invisible force drags her closer and closer to the trees and I'm losing my grip on her hand and then she seems to wake up and looks around her more confused than frightened.

And then her hand slips out of mine.

And then she's going backwards, faster and faster.

With a desperate lunge, I fling myself at her and tackle her to the ground and we end up in a tangled heap on a mossy bank.

"Hello, Rosa," says Alice, as though I've only just arrived.

"Hello, Alice," I say, because I can't think of anything else to say.

With a rushing sound, the force evaporates to nothing.

Chapter 64

In amongst all the weirdly odd and oddly weird things that have been happening around me lately, that last bit was officially scary.

I can cope with the mad fertility ritual in the woods thing. Just about. It's peculiar, it's bonkers but it's not frightening exactly unless you count the Emerging Madness of My Mother.

Then there's Megan's *Curse of the First Born Girls* story. That's strange too, but really, truthfully, thinking rationally (which I *can* do sometimes) this birthmark of mine might just be hereditary, mightn't it? One of those things that some members of the family have and others don't depending on their genes. It's just that a warped kind of legend has grown up around it.

Deborah's death is still a bit of a mystery but it's only a question of bludgeoning the truth out of Mum, and as for the grave, well, I might have been mistaken. Perhaps it wasn't there when I thought it was? Perhaps it *was* there when I thought it wasn't? Yep, I could have been mistaken. It has happened. Occasionally.

The train crash, the rainstorm. Who knows? Perhaps I was exaggerating, though it *does* seem odd that I exaggerate to *myself*. Why would I do that?

But this last occurrence... this is serious. Beyond my imagining. Out of my control. And I have no-one to turn to, no-one to ask, "What shall I do next?" No-one to say to me, "Do this and everything will be okay." Mum and Dad are worse than useless. There's only me. And that's scary. And it's scary because it's not about *me* anymore, it's about Alice.

"I'm telling you, it was just a gust of wind, Rosa," says Alice, reading my thoughts, and I wish I could believe her.

Keeping her close to me on the track towards home, she's happy and chatting and I don't know whether that's a good thing or a bad thing.

Even the sight of Bates stomping along towards us doesn't bother me. I hardly even look up, just put my arm round Alice's shoulder and draw her even closer in to my side, with much more important things to think about than a stroppy old gamekeeper.

I can't help smiling, even though my head is full to the point of exploding with worries, when, lurching up behind him, bounces the white van, bumping along the track, bits of metal dropping off and clouds of rust flying everywhere.

Bates gets level with the sign he just erected, stares at it with eyes bulging and with a roar rips it from the ground and launches it towards the approaching van. The word, "Wilding!" explodes from his mouth in a ball of fury.

The van hurtles ever nearer and doesn't stop. Alice gasps and her hand goes to her mouth in shock. I can't watch but I do anyway.

Bates, with remarkable agility for such a great clodhopper of a man, flings himself to one side and the van crunches to a halt right on top of where he would have been if he hadn't moved so quickly. Out leaps Caitlin and screams at him, "What have you gone and done with my dad?"

"What's your dad gone and done with my bleeding sign?" bellows Bates, picking it up and shoving it under her nose.

"I'm so not bothered about your stupid sign. Where's my dad?" Caitlin screeches into his face, well, more his chest because she's so much shorter than he is.

"Poaching game? Drinking cider? Looking for his van? How should I know?" Bates growls.

Caitlin's face crumples suddenly, all the bravado

gone out of her, and you can see she's fighting back tears and Bates begins to shuffle and mumble like a big kid.

"What's going on?" I ask, as Alice and I reach the two of them.

"Still searching for Dad," sniffs Caitlin.

Alice runs to Bates and takes the sign from him.

"Oh, *there* it is," she squeals with delight. "It said Wayland Woods, Private Property, Trespassers Will Be Prosecuted, didn't it? How funny!"

"So it was *you,*" he snarls.

"No wonder it faded away," she continues brightly.

Bates stares at her, bemused. He can face up to marauding wild animals, he can overcome savage gun-wielding poachers but innocent little girls like Alice are *way* too much for him to handle.

Alice frowns and says, "Well, really, how can woods be private?"

Chapter 65

We're dwarfed by Bates, us three girls, but I'm not in the slightest bit scared of him anymore.

I've discovered a brilliant strategy that you could use if you're scared of something. Find another thing that you're *even more* scared of then the first thing won't seem scary at all. (Actually, I'm thinking of writing a self-help book when I've finished writing this).

I say to Bates for possibly the tenth time, "If Alice says she didn't do it, then she didn't do it, *okay*?"

At last he holds his hands up in submission. "Fair enough. If you say so." Then he turns to Caitlin and says, "We should be getting that van back, miss."

Caitlin glowers. I expect she's feeling a bit like me, unused to the idea that perhaps Bates isn't so bad after all.

"I'll drive you," he offers. "Before you kill someone. Or get yourself arrested. Or your dad reports the van stolen."

The last bit produces a half-smile from Caitlin.

"Oh yeah, I'm sure he's on his way to the police station right now," she says. Bates pats her on the shoulder kindly and says, "He's not a bad man, your dad."

She shrugs him off, still not ready to let her defences down and I don't blame her after the way Bates has behaved. He doesn't give up though.

"Keeps me in work at any rate," he smiles. "Natural order of things. If there were no poachers, there'd be no need for gamekeepers, eh?"

This time Caitlin's face breaks into a *proper* smile and she looks so relieved I think maybe I'll wait to tell her about the wicked plans for Wayland Woods. It'll give me time to think of a way to put a stop to them.

I didn't know I cared that much.

I didn't know I cared that much until Alice and I are walking home. As we go, a pair of butterflies dance around her head and her smile is enchanting, which is naff, but my heart goes all gooey which is even more naff. Bleurrrrch!

Not for long.

From the middle of Wayland Woods we can hear machine noises, the loutish sound of men's voices calling out to each other, laughing, joking. There's nothing amusing about this. They shouldn't be there. It feels all wrong.

Alice and I look at each other and without a word we step back amongst the trees to see what's going on.

This time Wayland Woods makes us welcome, both of us.

This time, the trees hustle us along gently, wanting us to get somewhere, see something.

They *know*.

After a while, we come across a horrible sight. The horrible sight spelled S-I-G-H-T of a horrible site spelled S-I-T-E to be accurate, which I always try to be, marked out with poles and yellow and black stripy barrier tape like a crime scene.

Men in suits measure the area using piercing scarlet laser beams shooting out from little camera things on tripods. Other men in mucky overalls and hard hats paint huge crosses on to tree trunks in fluorescent orange paint. The trees seem to shudder as they do it. No, they don't *seem* to shudder, they *do* shudder.

I notice I'm shuddering as well. I suddenly feel very tiny.

Alice takes my hand and we watch in silence.

Across the other side of the site, we see the hare watching too.

Watching us.

Chapter 66

My Word Of The Day today is paradox. Or it might be enigma. Or both. Not sure. Whatever…

That's what I think about Wayland Woods, anyway. Sometimes ugly and oppressive; sometimes so beautiful I could cry. Sometimes threatening towards Alice, as though it wants to consume her; at other times welcoming, like it's ready to hug her.

I *do* know that I want to protect them, these woods. I *do* know that I must protect Alice. I *don't* know how I can do either.

If only I could understand.

At the moment, it's too hard even to understand what I'm trying to understand.

As I said, a paradox. Or an enigma. Or both. Not sure. Whatever…

Well, that was enlightening. Not. Allow me to change the subject.

Next day, Dad comes bounding down the stairs full of the joys of spring even though it's already summer. Under his arm he carries a roll of paper and announces to us that he's been busy, very busy.

I'm thinking, that makes a change, and Mum asks what it is he's been doing in the sort of way that you know she's not expecting to like what she will hear. She's right.

"It's sheer genius!" he says. "The best design I've ever created. Ever. I'm tickled pink. Tristan is going to *love* it!"

The question is…are *we* going to love it?

The answer is…no. A resounding no.

"Aren't you wondering what it is?" he asks, bubbling over with excitement.

"I am," says Alice, saving the day.

"Well," says Dad, unrolling the plans with a flourish. "I have devised the most marvellous tropical-rain-forest-themed indoor golf course which will sit perfectly next to Tristan's nine-hole classic design. All-weather golf. What do you think of *that*, girls? Isn't Daddy a clever chap?"

Daddy isn't.

"So, let me get this right," says Mum, her face taut. "You plan to destroy several acres of beautiful natural woodland in order to put up a large building with a fake forest inside it?"

"That's about the size of it!" says Dad, a huge grin plastered across his face.

"Isn't that a bit silly, Daddy?" says Alice.

Chapter 67

Luckily, Dad isn't ever put off when people throw cold water over his stupid ideas. That's how he made it big in graphic design, he tells us. (Until he lost his job). What, by having stupid ideas that people throw cold water over?

I'm only saying luckily because Dad is *so* excited about his tropical-rain-forest-themed indoor golf course that it seems quite horrible to be the one to tell him that it's possibly the very worst idea in the world. Ever.

Mum already did that after Alice's comment, so the spineless coward Rosa (me) didn't have to add anything. You can see by this that I'm true to my principles at all times.

Dad's eyes, just for a millisecond, told me that he was hurt, but he's like a non-stick frying pan in many ways. Well, *one* way. Things just slide off him. He hasn't got a handle and he's not made of metal.

So, the next minute he's all bouncy again and raring to get off to show his plans to Tristan. Maybe Tristan has more sense than my dad, but I doubt it.

My new role in The Family Cavanagh is that of sheep dog. Here's me, a little later, herding my dad and my kid sister towards The Manor House.

As for Mum, ever since Rhodri came bursting into the kitchen, she's hardly left the cottage, at least not in daylight hours. She must be frightened of running in to him. I would be.

Whatever the case, I think Mum is pretty negligent as mothers go. I mean, she gets her vulnerable young daughter involved in some loopy fertility ritual and then she can't even be bothered to go to The Preparation, which is where I'm headed now to make sure Alice is okay. Someone has to.

No doubt I'll have to look after Dad as well because he's quite incapable of taking care of himself where alcohol is concerned and I'm sure he and Tristan won't be drinking strawberry milkshake.

So, as I said - the family sheepdog.

Woof, woof!

Chapter 68

Dad carries a cardboard tube under his arm containing The Famous Plans.

He strides beside the perimeter wall towards the gates of The Manor House, bouncing along as though he has springs on his feet instead of shoes, so fast that Alice has to skip to keep up with him and my role as sheepdog is virtually redundant before it's even begun.

I'm sure I'll be much busier on the return journey.

"Oooh! I'm so excited about The Preparation," squeaks Alice. "I wonder what will happen? What do you think will happen, Daddy?"

"Search me, honeybun," says Dad. "Didn't Mummy say? Girlie stuff probably. You know the sort of thing."

"Not really," says Alice.

We can see Gloria through the gate, in a strange pose on the lawn, and Dad has difficulty with his jaw again.

She's wearing a wafty dress and you can see right through it to her underwear which is quite disgusting. Not "From-Marks-and-Spencer Disgusting," like mine, but "Because-You-Can-See-It-Through-Her-Dress Disgusting." She's got no shoes on either but that doesn't bother me. She stands, legs slightly apart, knees bent, eyes closed and then she breathes in and out deeply and does one of those pelvic thrust things.

Dad drops his cardboard tube.

Tristan races up beside her, even pinker than usual, and yells, "Don't you think you ought to wear something more substantial for our guests?"

"No," replies Gloria and then they see us and pretend everything is harmonious. Grown ups do that quite a lot.

We are whisked inside The Manor House and Dad

and Tristan beetle straight off to the study to look at the plans. As Gloria is escorting me and Alice up the grand staircase I can hear Tristan booming, "Splendid, absolutely splendid, old man!" And then saying more quietly, "Of course, we'll have to lose another slice of Wayland Wood…"

"We'll see about *that*," I think, without any idea what I can possibly do to stop it from happening. I think this is called The Optimism Of Youth.

"Come into my boudoir, daaaahling Alice," gushes Gloria and I follow them in like a leper. By this I don't mean my fingers and toes have dropped off, I just mean I am plainly unwelcome.

I have never seen such a bedroom.

There's a four poster bed and everything is festooned with silky drapes and on the bed are about a hundred squashy satin pillows and there are mirrors everywhere (even on the ceiling which strikes me as a bit odd) and there's a chandelier. A *chandelier*! A massive diamond-sparkly dangly chandelier! I don't mean to sound impressed. Material things Do Not impress me. Hardly at all.

"Are you a princess?" asks Alice, and Gloria's laugh is as silky as her drapes and probably her underwear too.

I retreat to a window seat and perch there, half-concealed by a curtain. It's the sort of thing that spurned girls do in Jane Austen novels so I may as well practice to prepare me for my life as a nobody.

There are no books for me to read, only some glossy magazines like *Vogue* and *Harper's Bazaar* that smell of sickly perfume. There's also a not-at-all flashy magazine called *Fertility Today* which I can't even bear to open in case of gory images of women's insides.

All I can do to entertain myself is watch The Preparation.

Chapter 69

In the middle of the room, Alice sits on an exotic chair carved with serpents and strange fruits. Gloria pampers her hair with languid strokes using an ivory-backed hairbrush and I start worrying about the poor tuskless elephants, wondering how they manage in the wild without them – and what do they use them for anyway apart from making hairbrushes?

It passes the time until, a lot of brushing later, Gloria holds a hand-mirror up to Alice's face and says, "See honey? See how it shines? Promise me you will always use rainwater to wash your hair?"

"The breezes and the sunshine and the soft refreshing rain," mumbles Alice, and Gloria says, "Excuse me?"

I know Alice has disappeared off into La-La Land again. It's what she does to hide from the real world when it all gets a bit wibbly-wobbly. I must try it. It certainly beats dealing with wibbly-wobbliness. In fact perhaps this could be Good Idea Number Two for my self-help book.

"Now, Alice!" says Gloria, so wrapped up in her own little schemes that she doesn't realise that Alice has temporarily left the building, "I have something very important to ask you."

"Ask and it shall be given," Alice murmurs. Gloria gives her what, for some reason, they call an old-fashioned look and clears her throat.

"Your monthly visitor, Alice?"

This inquiry must have penetrated deep into the mists of La-La Land because Alice immediately becomes alert then screws up her face in thought.

"Monthly visitor? Do I have one, you mean?" she asks.

"Exactly!" beams Gloria.

"I don't think so," says Alice after much deliberation. "Granny comes to stay every so often. Usually at Christmas."

Personally, I think Gloria would have achieved more if she'd just come out with it, like, "Alice, have you started your periods yet?"

Before she spontaneously combusts with fury at Alice's perversity, which isn't perversity at all but Gloria's too dumb to realise it, I say "No she hasn't started, if that's what you want to know," and Gloria practically oozes all over me with gratitude.

I think in many ways I prefer my leper status.

Alice's status is now transformed into that of Gloria's Barbie Doll Without The Boobs.

My opinion, if you're at all interested, is that if the only thing Gloria wants is a dolly to dress up in silly clothes then why can't she just *buy one*? I'm sure she can afford it. You can even get life-sized dolls if you're that bothered. I know this because I once saw Dad looking at some on the internet.

Rather to my disgust, Alice is quite enjoying being a Barbie doll so I don't bother to put a stop to it even though my patience is wearing very thin.

After lots of tedious faffing about with different costumes, Alice ends up wearing an over-large white dress which luckily isn't transparent or I would have something to say, and Gloria weaves wild flowers in her hair.

I must admit Alice looks quite pretty in a Flower Fairy sort of way if you like that style, which I don't. Gloria is in raptures, so many raptures that she might dissolve on the floor in a puddle of ecstasy. She stands Alice on the chair and walks around her gushing "Sublime! So innocent! So pure! So chaste!"

"Chased?" says Alice. "I don't want to be chased by

anyone, thank you very much," and Gloria laughs indulgently as though Alice has made the funniest joke. She really is very dim.

"We have to go now," says Alice suddenly, jumping off the chair.

Thank goodness for that.

Chapter 70

Getting away from Gloria isn't that simple. Once Alice has changed back into her own clothes, Gloria clings to her in a very nauseating way, whining, "But daaaahling, you *must* stay a little longer. We haven't *nearly* finished The Preparation."

"I feel perfectly prepared, thank you," states Alice, "And now we must stop Daddy from getting horribly drunk."

It's not easy for Gloria to stand up to such an argument, so reluctantly she releases Alice from her octopus-like tentacles and rushes over to a cabinet, a ghastly cabinet inlaid with mother-of-pearl, and brings out a small decorated box tied up with ribbons.

"I have a Special Present for you, Alice," she announces.

"I have quite a few boxes already, thank you," says Alice politely and I whisper to her that the present is probably inside the box so Alice takes it and puts it in her pocket.

"Aren't you going to open it?" wheedles Gloria. Really, she is far too syrupy for my taste.

Alice sighs and gets the box out of her pocket, unties the ribbons and lifts the lid. Inside is a lump of rock. Just what you always wanted. Actually, it's a bit better than a lump of rock, it's an egg-shaped piece of rosy pink quartz. (But basically it's a lump of rock).

"Oh, a lump of rock! How thoughtful!" says Alice.

"You must rub it," says Gloria.

"Must I?" says Alice.

"Yes, you must, at sunset and at moonrise, without fail. It will help," instructs Gloria, with half an eye on me, probably waiting for my howls of derision but I manage to keep them inside.

"Oh, you mean it will help with the secret thing that Megan says I'm not to mention to anyone?" says Alice, her eyes shining. Gloria nods.

The very mention of Megan's name makes me twitch. I dig Alice in the ribs and remind her that we are meant to be going.

Alice skips from the room clutching the egg and I follow at a more dignified pace because I'm fourteen and Gloria skips after me because she's forty at least and has lost all her self-respect.

Tristan and Dad are in the dining room smoking big fat cigars, which is unusual since Dad doesn't smoke. This time they are drinking champagne, proper posh stuff, not that sparkling wine you get at wedding receptions. They are on their second bottle.

"Daddy, you're drunk," says Alice.

"Just a little squiffy, sugarplum," splutters Dad in a cloud of cigar smoke, and he and Tristan laugh like drains, which is one of those expressions that people use and I don't know why because drains are not known for their laughing.

"The girls must join our celebrations," booms Tristan and he staggers to his feet and lurches towards the sideboard.

Gloria holds up her hand like a policeman at a traffic junction. "No she must not!" she shouts. "Her body is a temple."

She means Alice of course. No-one would describe my body as a temple.

"Spoilsport," slurs Tristan, tripping over his own feet and banging his nose on a cupboard. Alice taps Dad on the arm and tells him it's time to go now before he does anything as silly as that.

"Oh, you run along, sweetheart. I'll catch up with the two of you later," says Dad, and Tristan pours him another glass of champagne.

Chapter 71

In my best sheepdogly way, I herd Alice into the kitchen when we get home. Mum wears a tattered black dress and stirs a large cauldron of strawberry jam with an enormous wooden spoon. I glance around fearfully hoping not to find a broomstick propped in a dark corner somewhere. There is a mop but I don't think that counts.

"Hubble, bubble, toil and trouble," says Alice. So she noticed too.

"There you are!" Mum says unnecessarily. Maybe I should give her a few lessons in The Art Of Intelligent Conversation.

"Yes, here we are," I reply. "Dad looked after us so well that we can all stop worrying, can't we?"

Sarcasm. Waste of breath.

"That's good!" says Mum brightly. "Where is he?"

Alice dances around the kitchen burbling something about men and girls coming and going like moths among the whisperings and the champagne.

I wonder for the millionth time how all this stuff finds its way into Alice's head then I say, spitefully, "Dad's still with Tristan and he made us walk home on our own."

(Not that I care. I'd rather walk home without him any day but he is meant to be A Responsible Adult)

"How lovely!" says Mum.

I give up.

When we go to bed, Dad still isn't home.

I lie there wishing I had someone to talk to about everything. It could be Caitlin. She would understand but then she's in the same sort of position as me, with a dad who drinks a lot, except her dad drinks cider not champagne. I think this illustrates the difference in our social classes but then it's Tristan's champagne that Dad drinks not his own so perhaps it doesn't count. And Caitlin doesn't have a mum at home to worry about things for her, but then neither do I. Well, I have a mum at home but she is entirely unreliable.

And now it seems I have a dad at home as well and he's entirely off his face, crashing about in the garden singing at the top of his sorry, drunken voice

"...Whack for my daddy-o
Whack for my daddy-o
There's whiskey in the jar..."

Then he trips over a flowerpot or something and lands flat on his face and I can hear the

KERTHUMP

...all the way from the garden and the singing is replaced by horrible swearing. It might have been funny if it wasn't such a sad reflection of The State Of My Parents.

"Can't you sleep either?" asks Alice, after a while, and when I confess that I can't she says in that case she will read me a story and my heart plummets THOINK to the bottom of my ribcage because I know exactly which story it will be. She whips her exercise book out from under her pillow and I close my eyes and wish ears had lids too. (After the self-help book, maybe I'll write something about Unusual Ideas For Plastic Surgery).

I won't bore you with the bits of the story you already know but I will bore you with the bit that I hadn't heard, the bit after Elinor has stolen the baby. It makes me wonder if there is perhaps something in this legend idea after all.

The Curse Of The First Born Girls

(the interesting bit that comes later)

Aodhán cried aloud that all the world might hear, 'I know it better than any man living; her family cursed shall be by this deed.'

The old crone turned to Elinor and said 'Your man tells you truth. I warn you well, your family shall ever be cursed by your dishonour. From this day forth the firstborn girls, each and every one, will be blemished such that men will turn away from them with loathing.

Do you see what I mean?

Chapter 72

After that I must have fallen asleep but I wish I hadn't due to the horrible nightmare.

Elinor is in it, wandering alone through Wayland Woods. One side of her is lit by moonlight and she's so utterly beautiful, radiantly beautiful like an angel. But then she turns and even though it's a nightmare I can't bear to look because the other side of her face is hideous scarlet and swollen and knotted with veins and then Elinor changes into Deborah and she's outside the Wildings' cottage staring and staring at something as though her heart will break and I don't know what it is and then she's tearing at her own face with her fingernails, like a wild animal, and there's blood pouring down her cheek and then she's running, running, running, screaming... and then I wake up.

Silence.

It takes me a while to realise it was a dream, a bit like when you get off a really fast fairground ride and the world is still spinning. Then I put my hand to my face and it comes away warm and wet. In the cracked mirror, by the light of the moon I can see that I've scratched my birthmark until it bleeds.

Chapter 73

I'm woken in the morning by the annoying sound of Alice humming. When I open my eyes, she's sitting up in bed stroking the rose quartz egg and I tell her she's weird. Then I remember my face and realise that Alice is very much kinder than I am because if anyone's weird it's got to be me.

In the mirror, the sight of me hasn't improved. If I could describe it as a kind of fashion statement, it might be abattoir meets aspiring rock chick. Daylight is considerably worse than moonlight for revealing the mess I've made of myself and it makes me groan with self-disgust. What have I *done*? I struggle enough to get my make-up on smoothly over my ordinarily horrible ugly face and now…?

"You could use bits of tissue like Daddy does when he cuts himself shaving," says Alice helpfully.

Oh yes, that would be very stylish. I'll just have to stay in my room for the next three weeks, that's all.

Mum has other ideas. She's invited Gloria and Megan round for yet another meeting about The Ritual and for some reason, she wants me there. Probably to wait on them hand and foot so Gloria feels more at home in the presence of peasants.

Alice goes down to breakfast and it doesn't take long for Mum to start screeching up the stairs, "Rosa! Keith! How many times?"

Oh yes, Dad. Perhaps Mum wants him to be a butler. I expect he's feeling super well this morning, with absolutely no headache at all. I can hear him groaning into the toilet which serves him right, if you ask me.

After a bit, there's a pounding of Impatient Mother's Feet on the stairs and I just manage to lock the bedroom door before she gets to it and knocks. Actually, to say she knocks is another of those euphemism things. She hammers on the door so hard that the cracked mirror falls off the wall and breaks into a thousand pieces and I'm quite glad.

"Rosa, they'll be here in a minute," she says quite pleasantly, in a first attempt to coax me out.

My response is "Yay!" (This is not meant to indicate enthusiasm. You just have to say it in the right way)

Mum's second attempt: "Won't you come down and say hello?"

My response: "No thanks."

Mum's third attempt: "There's no need to hide yourself away."

My response: "No, you're absolutely right, mother. How silly of me!"

"Good girl!" says Mum, scenting victory.

How wrong can one mum be? Then she goes to the other bedroom and yells "Rise and shine, Keith!"

I think she's quite lucky not to get a smack in the mouth even though I am totally against domestic violence.

Chapter 74

I station myself at the window to see what transpires. It might take my mind off my face. I have plastered the sore bit with Soothing Cream For Skin Irritations so now I look like half a clown.

Gloria has a posh car. I don't know why I'm surprised. It's one of those sporty jobs, metallic gold, roof down and even so not a hair is out of place on Gloria's head though it does look a bit stiff like she's fixed it in position with wallpaper paste. She extends an elegant leg out of the car door and slides out. At least she's wearing proper clothes today so you can't see her knickers. She looks at the cottage with distaste which she quickly transforms into pleasure as Mum comes running out to meet her, dressed like a milkmaid.

"Sally, you look...awesome!" she oozes. "And what a daaahling little cottage!"

I stick two fingers down my throat.

Gloria continues, "I am simply *dying* to see that precious girl of yours."

She treads carefully across the lawn in ridiculous high heels, with Mum following in her wake carrying all her bags. How humiliating! They disappear inside and then there's the sound of Gloria gushing all over Alice. How even more humiliating.

Then Megan is there in the garden though I didn't see her walking down the lane. She looks straight up at the window, her eyes glinting, and it makes me gasp and draw back but it's too late, she's already seen me.

Alice bursts out of the back door, probably to get away from the danger of being suffocated in clouds of Gloria's exotic perfume, and she flings herself at Megan, squealing, "Will it be soon? Please let it be soon!"

"Sooner than you imagine, child," replies Megan, and Alice dances with delight while Megan sneers up at me.

"It's so hard to keep it secret," says Alice, pirouetting on the lawn.

"Perhaps it may happen within the week, if the signs are right," says Megan and takes a fleeting look up at my window. I'm sure it's to make certain I've heard.

"I ask of thee, beloved night, swift be thine approaching flight!" cries Alice, spinning so fast it makes me dizzy just to watch her, then they go inside.

Within the week? What will happen within the week?

I'm plunged into deep thoughts of sisterly concern so I don't notice another person approaching the cottage and when I do, I almost keel over with the shock of it and the fear that my face has been seen because that person is the last person I would want to see my face like this and that person is Kieron.

Chapter 75

I can just see the garden gate out of one eye by peering round the window frame an inch or two. I choose the side not covered in soothing cream.

Kieron is wearing…oh, I don't want to tell you what he's wearing because that makes me sound like I'm interested, but he looks okay and his hair flops over his eyes and he pushes it back with one hand and his eyes are still green, green enough for me to see from here with only one of my eyes. He vaults over the garden gate without opening it and I can't decide whether that is athletic or posey and come to the conclusion that it's a bit of both.

Then I'm holding my breath waiting and it all comes out in a whoosh when he strides to the door and gives it an energetic thump and it vibrates right through me like my heart beat.

THUMP THUMP THUMP.

Then I hold my breath again, not even knowing why, because my heart's beating so loudly that holding my breath isn't exactly going to help me in my attempt to remain unnoticed and there's muffled talking going on downstairs and then Mum shouts, "Rosa, you have a visitor!" and I jump into bed and pull the blankets right over my head.

Darkness. The relief of it. Then footsteps on the stairs and there's a tapping on the door and it's Alice and she whispers, "It's Kieron, Rosa. He's brought back your boot."

And I don't answer then she calls down the stairs, "I'm afraid she's fast asleep."

I love Alice sometimes.

Retreating footsteps and more muffled voices and then the back door goes again and I just can't help it and get out of bed and go to the window and Kieron is gazing up at it so I have to duck out of sight very quickly. And he stands there. And I'm holding my breath again and he looks kind of disappointed but I expect that's me imagining things and then he shrugs and turns to go.

And I scrub my face with a flannel so hard that it makes me cry with the pain of it and it's not as if I can ever rub my birthmark away.

Chapter 76

I get it in my head that I must see Caitlin. It's either that or my head explodes. My head exploding would solve the problem of the birthmark once and for all but is not a practical solution. Of course, the idea of seeing Caitlin has a number of difficulties attached to it. These are:

1. I've got to get past everyone in the kitchen without them seeing me
2. Caitlin's dad hates me and *his* head would explode if I went anywhere near their cottage again
3. Caitlin might not be at home and if she isn't I don't know where she'll be
4. Kieron might be there and if he is I would die.

I know what you're thinking. I know you're thinking that I've suddenly got this burning urge to see Caitlin because then there might be a teensy-weensy itsy-bitsy chance of seeing Kieron again. I would just like to inform you that YOU ARE MISTAKEN.

I want to see Caitlin because I so desperately need someone to talk to and she's the only person I can think of. Which doesn't sound very flattering towards Caitlin but I don't mean it like that.

The other thing is me not thinking of myself but of Other People and The Environment. (I *am* capable of weighty thoughts, you see). I have to warn Caitlin about her cottage and the imminent destruction of Wayland Woods and maybe together we can do something to stop it.

Difficulty Number One, getting out of the cottage unseen, should be relatively easy as we have a front door as well as a back door. Duh! It's just that it's never used and has about a hundred bolts on it, as if anyone would ever want to burgle us.

I do the best job possible with my face then creep down the stairs and when I'm nearly at the bottom someone else arrives at the back door and to my horror it's The Vicar.

I freeze. Not literally because it's quite warm.

The inside kitchen door is open just a crack and through it I can see Alice standing on a chair in that dress again, and Mum and Gloria are swarming all over her pulling bits tighter here and there and pinning them into place. I can't see Megan but The Vicar is practically drooling over Alice.

"*What* a pretty little girl you are," he says in his slimy awful voice.

"Isn't she just, my precious Alice!" coos Gloria.

Since when did Alice belong to Gloria?

Alice smiles one of her winning smiles. I wish she wouldn't encourage them as they don't need it.

The Vicar goes on, "So when do I get to meet...Rosa, isn't it?"

I think I will shrivel up and die on the spot. And what a freaking liar he is because he already *has* met me, hasn't he? Mum and Alice exchange anxious glances and Megan comes into view in the crack in the door, grinning unpleasantly.

"I imagine Rosa must be quite as pretty as you, Alice?" says The Vicar.

Mum starts to answer slowly, "She..."and Alice takes over when Mum can't quite bring herself to speak the truth.

"She *is* as pretty as me, isn't she Mummy?" says Alice, then she smiles at Megan and says, "At least, she very soon will be, won't she?"

Megan's eyes narrow and she puts a finger to her lips. Alice's hand goes to her mouth.

Well, forget the pigging front door. I burst through the kitchen and outside before anyone has the chance to utter a single word.

Chapter 77

As luck would have it, and that is a rare occurrence in my miserable existence, Caitlin's on the track leading to her cottage.

"What's happened to your face?" she says, straight to the point.

"Allergic to hedgehogs," I say, thinking on my feet, and I wait for her to howl with incredulous laughter but she says, "Ouch!" and that's that. Phew! I'll have to remember that one for future use. And my self-help book.

She's concealing something behind her back and shuffling from foot to foot so I ask her what's up. She says "Nothing," but her cheeks go bright scarlet which clashes badly with her hair and then she says, "I'm going to post a letter, if you must know."

Like, big deal.

"To my mum," she mumbles and then I understand. Or at least, I think I do.

"I've asked her to come home," she says. "Told her we miss her." Her face is all crumpled and I give her a hug which is not in my nature because I'm someone who prides herself on being ultra cool and detached but must be losing my grip for some reason.

I don't mention the fact that she told me her mother is a slag. Neither do I mention that having a mother at home doesn't necessarily mean that you are properly cared for because I'm certainly not.

We set off back the way I came, alongside meadows so alive with wild flowers that you couldn't help but feel joyful and as we go I tell her the worrying news about Wayland Wood, hoping it won't tip her completely over the edge what with her already jumbled up feelings about contacting her mum.

It doesn't seem to because she livens up immediately and says "Bloody bastards!" which just about sums it up.

"We shall go to The Manor House," I announce boldly, "And we will persuade Tristan that he's morally bankrupt with no thought for future generations what with him and Gloria wanting a baby and everything."

"And failing that," says Caitlin, "We shall become Eco-Warriors!"

I think it's the heat getting to us, frying our brains, because we don't usually speak such pretentious drivel. I mean, who do we think we *are*? It's not that we don't care about all these things, by the way, just that it's deluding ourselves big time to imagine that we can stand in the way of progress and People in Authority.

By this time, we've reached the post box which nestles in a falling down stone wall on the outskirts of the village. Probably the letters just stay in it until they crumble to dust but I don't mention this to Caitlin, being in a considerate frame of mind.

She takes a deep breath and after a moment's hesitation, she gives the letter a quick kiss and slips it through the slot and it lands in the base of the box with a whispery plop.

"There," she says, "That's done. Now all I've got to do is to wait forever for her not to reply."

"I'm sure she'll reply," I say encouragingly, inside my head wondering why Caitlin's so bothered. Adults can't be trusted. I used to be so full of hope when I was younger a few days ago. Better distract her so as not to infect her with The Cynicism That Comes With Maturity.

"We must make a decision about what we do next in our plans to foil the dastardly destruction of our heritage."

To my surprise she says, "Let's go back to my

place. I think we should tell Dad."

A whole lot of What Ifs? leap into my head uninvited. I think my skull must be quite transparent because Caitlin seems to have no bother at all in reading my mind.

"Kieron's gone fishing," she says.

Chapter 78

As we get closer to the cottage, my stomach starts doing somersaults and back flips which I put down to the possible closeness of Rhodri after the dire warning he gave to me such a short time ago.

I keep on saying to Caitlin, "I don't think this is a good idea, in fact I think this is a rubbish idea," but she is totally unperturbed and tells me not to worry, she can sort her dad out any day.

And there in the sky above the trees is the plume of smoke from the cottage chimney. But why it is they have a fire when it's blazing hot in the middle of summer? Perhaps it's just for effect and there's no fire at all?

We round the last corner and we're there and the first thing I see is Rhodri and for a moment he looks like Kieron because they're quite similar only Rhodri is older. Obviously.

If only Caitlin was a bit bigger so I could hide behind her. I'm only telling you this because I promised myself to be brutally honest about my feelings. Just don't go away with the impression that I'm a wuss. At the moment I don't look at my best face-wise and it's doubtful Rhodri will be convinced by the hedgehog allergy explanation.

Rhodri is not in a state to notice anything very much and he's not even drunk as far as I can tell because he's still as a photograph by the front porch. When you've had too much to drink you mostly sway, as I know from my long experience of observing Dad.

Rhodri is, however, staring into the depths of a pint glass of cider as though he might find the answer to some very important question there. He's also crying.

Caitlin looks at me and it's obvious that even she's

beginning to question the wisdom of springing me upon him unawares.

"I'll wait here, if it's all the same to you," I say, and squat down out of sight behind an ancient tractor. She gives me a grateful smile that's followed by a weary sigh then she walks towards her dad. I suppose this is why people have children, to take care of them when they're in a bit of a state.

All of a sudden Rhodri lets out a despairing cry and throws the cider out of the glass in a shower of golden droplets all over the ground.

"Dad," cries Caitlin and belts over to him but he shoves her out of the way and she stands there helplessly watching him charge in and out of the cottage each time emerging with more flagons of cider which he empties out on the ground and all you can hear, apart from his crashing about, is glugging sounds.

On the whole I think it's a good thing that at last he has seen the error of his ways but it is excruciatingly embarrassing to witness.

"Shall I help, Dad?" Caitlin asks at one point, but he looks right through her blinded by tears and carries on with his emptying.

I honestly don't think he properly takes in that Caitlin is there. What he reminds me of most is something I saw on TV a while ago and I could only watch for a few minutes before I hid behind the settee, hands over my ears. It was a bullfight and the poor wounded animal was skewered in the neck and shoulders with barbed sticks and he was roaring and charging round the ring, eyes clouded with the pain and don't expect me ever to go on holiday to Spain or even eat tapas because *I won't*.

And Rhodri is shouting something now and what he's shouting is, "I didn't mean to hurt you Deb, honest I didn't, but I said it, I said it and I can never take it back, that if you were half as pretty as your sister, I might have given you a second glance."

Chapter 79

WHOOMPH! That's the sound of all my feelings bursting from my body just as though I've fallen over with a thump and knocked the wind out of myself. That's exactly what it's like. Things are becoming horribly clear and I think that it's time for me to get out of here. Quickly.

In front of the cottage, Caitlin hugs a sobbing Rhodri and it's a pitiful sight and she's saying, "What are you talking about, Dad? Tell me, tell me."

I know what he's talking about.

I stand up to go, poking my head up above the old tractor wanting to wave goodbye to Caitlin so at least she knows I'm leaving, but that's a big mistake because when I do Rhodri catches sight of me and lets out an ear-damaging scream and backs away into the porch in terror as though he's seen another ghost, which I suppose in a way he has.

Caitlin shakes her head at me frantically, warning me to keep away, as if I would voluntarily want to go near Rhodri ever again, then she disappears after him inside the cottage and I disappear inside my head and walk back through Wayland Woods.

Right, so a long, long time ago my best friend's dad has so horribly upset my auntie Deborah because of the way she looks that she ends up drowning herself? And now there's me. And I'm just like Deborah with the birthmark. And I have a pretty little sister the same as Deborah had my mum for her sister. And then there was that time at the river with Another Person that I'm not going to mention...

And...

I'm not going to drown myself, by the way.

I expect you had worked that out already. If I had

drowned myself you wouldn't be reading *this*.

I'm not going to drown myself but I'm certainly not in the mood to go home to see my pretty little sister and my mum who is somehow involved in all this much more than simply having been Deborah's pretty little sister or why would she still be so upset and not visit the grave? That's if there *is* a grave.

I'm not going home. Instead I wander the countryside like a lost soul, making sure to keep well away from any rivers or lakes or ponds. This is not in case I suddenly feel the urge to throw myself into the water with my pockets filled with pebbles. This is in case there's Someone I Don't Want To See fishing there.

I vaguely think of going to the Manor House and confronting Tristan DeVere but quite honestly haven't the heart for that at the moment. As it turns out, it would have been a wasted journey.

Chapter 80

Wayland Woods is a comforting place to be today, a friend, and I expect you're thinking "First she gets matey with a grave and now it's a bunch of trees, she really is an odd girl and best avoided at all costs." But you try it with the things and places. They are so much more reliable than people, any day.

I find myself a patch of sun-speckled grass and lie down in it and never mind the creepy-crawlies and it could have been heaven if my mind wasn't working overtime and won't stop even for the shortest comfort break.

To distract myself, I close my eyes and make a list of all the different noises that there are around and about me and I just get to Number Fifteen, the sound of me scratching my leg where I have been bitten by a Killer Midge, when a louder, unnatural sort of rumbling makes me sit up with a start.

At the same moment a cloud passes over the sun and I come out in goose pimples all over my arms so I guess my friend, Wayland Woods, is telling me something and that is to stop obsessing about my own silly worries and get myself over to the source of the new noise and Do Something About It.

It doesn't take me long to realise that it's coming from The Horrible Site. When I get there it's grown about twenty times larger overnight and there's miles of barrier tape flapping yellow and black and ugly against the natural greens of the woodland and dozens of burly men doing burly men jobs with bits of chunky machinery all painted bright yellow and orange and black as well to make them look powerful and manly.

(Someone should pass a law that all mechanical tools must be painted pale pink or lilac. I bet *that* would stop them playing their manly games.)

I'm ashamed, sure this increase in activity has something, everything, to do with my dad's plans for the tropical-rain-forest-themed indoor golf course and I'm proved right when I get up close and overhear two of the men having a good moan to each other.

These men aren't so burly and wear smart suits, which is ridiculous when you're in the middle of a wood in the baking heat of the sun so I expect they are Senior Managers, the sort of people who don't do any of the work but watch everyone else doing it instead and make helpful comments.

One of them growls to the other, "Sodding bulldozers coming in at dawn tomorrow and now His Royal Highness wants to change the sodding plans to include a sodding indoor golf course."

Someone should buy him a dictionary. There are sure to be more adjectives in it.

Tomorrow, though? Tomorrow! That doesn't give me much time, does it?

And when he says His Royal Highness he points over to another part of the site and there is Tristan pinkly important with a clipboard and Bates standing right next to him looking sombre so I'd better get over there and find out what's happening and confront them.

I can do it.

Maybe.

As I'm creeping round the perimeter keeping myself hidden in the undergrowth I almost bump smack into two enormous lumberjacks who *are* burly and they are the ones doing all the work judging by their brawny arms and dirty overalls without wanting to be at all stereotypical about Labouring Types.

They're walking round and round one enormous tree trunk with bemused expressions on their faces and one of them says in a deep husky voice, "You're going barmy you are, mate."

The other one replies in an even gruffer voice, "No I'm flaming well not. I put a cross on that tree yesterday, as sure as eggs is eggs."

Oh, those hideous fluorescent daubs Alice and I saw. The ones that marked the trees ready for destruction and the agonised shuddering it seemed to cause. And the trees all around me are shaking again, but this time I'm pretty sure it's with laughter. Yes, it's insane. I know. It's insane or *I'm* insane. Or both.

Across the site there are various vans parked and a mobile site office, an unsightly box all metal and glass and trailing cables, and my eye is drawn to them in horrified fascination as fluorescent orange crosses appear on their sides as if by magic. Yes I blink, yes I rub my eyes and all that stuff you do when you're puzzled, but the crosses keep on appearing and I'm the only one who notices.

And the trees shake and shake and it makes me laugh too.

"Wind's picking up," one of the lumberjacks mutters.

Chapter 81

I get round as far as Tristan DeVere and he's waving Dad's plans, I'm *sure* they're Dad's plans, under the nose of another suited man carrying a leather briefcase and a rolled up newspaper as though he's just stepped off the 6.02 train from London Victoria and is not under an oak tree in the heart of Rural Somerset.

Tristan slaps him on the back and smarms, "Jolly good show! I say, keep this between you, me and the gatepost pro tem, won't you? Wouldn't want to upset the local yokels, now would we?"

Then he guffaws with laughter.

The trees fall silent.

Bates stands to one side, about to be sick by the look of him, and I'm positive he notices me in the bushes but if he does, he doesn't let on.

"Now, Bates!" booms Tristan, and Bates steps over to him and I wouldn't have been surprised if he had tugged his forelock or bowed subserviently but suppose Tristan does pay his wages.

"More security you're wanting is it?" asks Bates.

"Absolutely!"

Bates shuffles uncomfortably and mutters, "And the pheasants? They're very close to the site…"

And I hate Tristan and everything he stands for even more when he says dismissively "They were bred to be shot…" Then he gives Bates a piercing, challenging look and finishes… "So shoot them."

For a brief moment I'm wondering if I might have misheard Bates when he was talking and he didn't refer to pheasants but peasants. We're very close to the Wildings' cottage on this side of the site.

I *can't* have misheard, can I?

But…
Now is the moment!
Now is the moment to leap out of the bushes and confront Tristan DeVere and tell him that what he plans to do is a heinous crime and an assault on all that is natural and that he's a money-grabbing fiend who should be locked up and then we will throw away the key and never mind the fact that I'm only fourteen, I Always Stand Up For What Is Right and I Won't Be Diverted From My Path of Righteousness.

Instead, I slink off into the undergrowth and make my way home.

Chapter 82

Sticking to your principles is never easy especially not when your stomach is telling you that it's a long way past midday and isn't it about time you filled it up with something good to eat? If I knew more about country ways I could pick berries from hedgerows and make nourishing soups out of mushrooms and tree bark but as it is I am likely to poison myself and die a horrible death because I can't tell a Rosehip from a Deadly Nightshade. That is a bit of an exaggeration but you can see what I'm getting at.

There is still time to take positive action about The Horrible Site. Not *much* time admittedly, but there is time.

One of my favourite quotes ever is something that Anne Frank of The Diary said and she is one of my role models although I'm not planning to die as young, about how wonderful it is that nobody need wait a single moment before starting to improve the world.

Now I'm wishing I hadn't mentioned that because it makes me seem like a waste of space because I *am* waiting to improve the world. Not just a single moment but lots of moments stuck together. Forget I said it. That would be best.

I enter the kitchen, nose in air, trying to pretend I hadn't stormed out of it like a spoilt brat only a few hours earlier even though there were very good reasons, as you know. I needn't have worried. No-one made any comment. They probably didn't even notice my dramatic exit me being a person of so little significance.

By this time, my stomach is positively screaming at me. Well, negatively screaming at me to be more precise. Stuff like, "You inconsiderate girl. Why don't you look after me properly?"

I search in one cupboard after another in a desperate hunt for cornflakes and Alice knows what I'm after without being told, goes straight to the larder and brings out a packet. Next I'm wondering where the bowls are kept and Alice puts one into my hand then trots off to get some milk. Smartypants. Mind-reader. But she has her uses.

Then Mum pauses in her endless task of scraping burnt bits off the oven and by some miracle the fog has cleared from her brain and she sees that I'm there which is good because of me wanting to talk to her about Deborah when I can get her on her own. She also sees my ravaged face which is less advantageous. "Oooh, that looks nasty," she says.

Thanks, Mum.

Her voice hesitant, she offers Megan's special powers to create, just for me, a Magic Healing Potion, proving that my mum is able to manage a few seconds of rational thought in one go.

Before I have time to say, "Not while I still have breath in my body!" in my best scathing manner, Alice pipes up "No need, because *tonight*..." then she stops any other words from coming out of her mouth by pinching her lips together with her fingers.

"Yes, Mum," I say emphatically, though I'm sure I already know the answer to the question I'm about to ask and I'm just testing her in a cruel way, "What *exactly* were those people doing here this morning?"

"They were getting me ready," says Alice.

"Getting Alice ready for *what* precisely, Mum?"

"Errrm," Mum mumbles, her eyes shifting to look anywhere but at me, "Alice is taking part in a sort of... a play."

Then she rushes out into the garden. She can't escape from The Inquisition that easily even if she thinks she can, but first I must eat my cornflakes.

Chapter 83

My stomach is slightly less offended at its lack of nutrition with the cornflakes swashing around inside it. I make my way outside and of course, Dad has to be in the garden too, doesn't he? So yet again there's no chance of talking to Mum, just when I had summoned up all my courage. As if.

The heat out there is pulsating, oppressive. Dad lounges in a deckchair with a sun hat over his face. Mum weeds the garden like a mad woman and this is called Displacement and was invented by Mr. Freud as a way of taking your mind off other things though I don't expect he intended anyone to go about it by massacring dandelions in a flowerbed.

I expect the other things she is trying to displace are:

1. That her daughter Rosa (me) is dangerously close to finding out the truth about her shady past
2. That she is about to expose her younger daughter (Alice) to the idiotic activities of some sort of insane woodland cult
3. That she is married to an indolent wastrel (Dad) who spends his time devising plans that will ultimately destroy the world as we know it.

They are busily arguing about point number 3 as I arrive.

"The golf complex is *not* destruction, Sal, it's creation, I'm telling you," insists Dad from under his sun hat.

"But all those beautiful trees..." says Mum. With this small observation, she manages to crawl a couple of notches up in my estimation.

"Talking of trees," Dad goes on, "When *is* the right

time to plant them?"

"About thirty years ago," snaps Mum and stomps off to the other end of the flowerbed to engage in further displacement activity with some unsuspecting nettles.

"I meant tropical trees," says Dad, "You know, bananas, coconut, palm, that sort of thing. For my tropical theme."

A gust of not-at-all tropical English wind comes out of nowhere and blows his hat over the fence.

"What did you want to go and do that for?" he says to me crossly, leaping to his feet to retrieve it.

Yes, I've said it before but I'm going to say it again.

I give up.

Chapter 84

Alice is meant to be resting ready for the big night and I'm quite happy to stay with her in our bedroom. It's cooler in there and it's also as far away from Mum and Dad as it's possible to be and still be inside. They haven't stopped arguing yet.

Alice fixes a brand new second-hand mirror to the wall above the wash basin. It's not at the top of my list of Things I'd Like In The Bedroom. I was quite happy when the other mirror shattered.

I sit cross-legged on my bed cradling The Boot. Don't ask me why I'm doing this. My other boot which has not been fished out of the river by Kieron Wilding is not nearly as appealing, for some reason. The River Boot is still rather damp despite the sizzling hot weather and the fact that I've been cradling it for the past two hours, which hasn't gone unnoticed.

"I don't think that'll work," says Alice and I grunt nonchalantly which is my way of saying shut up, but she doesn't take the hint.

"I don't think that'll work as a way of drying your boot, holding it like that," she continues.

"I suppose not," I reply, cradling it some more.

"Because you have been holding it almost from the moment he brought it back, haven't you? And it's still not dry," she finishes.

Kid sisters should be seen and not heard.

It's rather a relief to me that, just at that moment, Mum calls up the stairs "Are you resting, Alice?"

Alice shouts "Yes!" and I shout "No!" simultaneously and then I add, "Liar, liar, pants on fire!"

She tells me she's too excited to rest and I tell her she's nuts. This is not meant unkindly even though she is.

"So," I go on, to deflect attention further from The Boot and my cradling of it, "Am I going to enjoy this…play of yours?"

"We didn't think you'd be coming," says Alice blushing. Alice *never* blushes. People who blush are embarrassed about something and I've always believed that Alice is incapable of this because of Her Condition only letting her be thoroughly honest about absolutely everything.

"Of course I'll be coming," I say.

"I didn't think you'd want to. With your face like that, I mean," says Alice, blushing even more furiously.

"Well, stuff your stupid little play then," I say, and Alice goes very quiet.

The thing is, I know perfectly well what's going on here. It's Megan who doesn't want me to be there, not Alice at all. Alice loves me to be wherever she is. I know that. This is worrying in the extreme.

Then Alice says in a tiny little voice, "Megan told me the cure for your face won't work if you're there."

"Listen Alice," I say seriously, "I thought all this nonsense in the woods, this ritual thing, was to do with Gloria and her dodgy womb."

"Ah," says Alice, "That's what everyone is *meant* to think but it's not that at all. Megan says I must take part in The Ritual or your face will always be… like it is. It's a secret so I shouldn't have told you."

Then she adds, "Please promise me you won't come tonight."

"Of course I won't come, if that's what you want," I say to Alice.

"Yeah right," I say to myself. "If Megan thinks I'm going to fall for that one she's got another think coming."

Chapter 85

Some time later, the bitter arguments from downstairs have subsided so it might be safe to venture into the kitchen for another bowl of cornflakes. There won't be any dinner cooked tonight, that's for sure, with Mum so engrossed in The Ritual, gathering strange herbs from the garden and grinding exotic spices with a pestle and mortar. Or perhaps that *is* dinner? I decide to stick with the cornflakes.

Dad is slouched over the kitchen table, glass in one hand, eyes glazed over and a tiny dribble of saliva trickling from one corner of his mouth. Mmmm, very attractive. I'll have to check my birth certificate to make sure he really *is* my dad. I can't believe we can possibly be from the same gene pool.

He's busy designing signs for the golf complex, each one sickeningly embellished with cartoon drawings of palm trees. I expect that was what the argument was all about. That or the excessive intake of alcohol.

But then, to my surprise, while I'm trying to be unobtrusive in the corner tucking into a huge bowl of cereal, Mum offers him another drink. She *hates* him drinking, probably as much as I do. I give her a withering look. So very effective, my withering looks are. Without waiting for Dad's answer, she snatches the glass from the table and pours him a very large whisky. A VERY large whisky.

Dad can hardly get his words out. He squints at Mum out of one bloodshot eye and says, "What are you trying to do to me, Sal? Render me unconscious so you can have your wicked way with my compliant body?"

Mum giggles hysterically. I would giggle hysterically in her position.

A couple of minutes later he's already about half way through the whisky and his drawings are getting very scribbly indeed when his head slumps down on the table and he starts snoring horribly.

"Good," says Mum, "He was threatening to come to The Ritual. We wouldn't want that, would we?"

"Wouldn't we? I thought you'd be keeping away too."

Mum can't look at me. She says nothing, which says a lot more than saying something.

"Because of Rhodri," I go on. Sometimes I can be so insistent.

"He's not going to be there," she mumbles, and then, before I have a chance to dig deeper, blurts out, "Is Alice ready? Are you?"

"I'm not coming."

She looks a tiny bit taken aback but as she doesn't beg me to change my mind it's obvious I'm not wanted. It's quite surprising she didn't knock me out with alcohol as well as Dad, just to make sure.

Now is the moment, isn't it? Again.

Mum bustles around the kitchen, putting weird concoctions into jam jars and tying up bunches of dried flowers with twine then laying them in a wicker basket. And Dad is unconscious. I take a deep breath. No words come out of my mouth. Coward! Take another deep breath and…

"Mum, what did Rhodri do to Deborah?"

There, I said it.

I know she's heard because she stops her bustling, her back to me. She doesn't say a word. The silence hangs in the air.

"Mum?"

She speaks very slowly, without turning around.

"It wasn't Rhodri. It was me."

Then Alice bursts into the kitchen squealing, "The

time has come, the walrus said!"

Oh, Alice.

It is kind of ironic that what the walrus said was "The time has come... to talk of many things..."

Mum does turn round then and her eyes glisten with tears.

Chapter 86

I watch them go from the bedroom window.

Alice stands in the middle of the lawn in a cloak of emerald green, gazing up at me. It might be my imagination but…I don't know why I keep on writing that because it isn't my imagination, it's really happening…definitely… around her feet a ring of grass grows, creeping upwards so it becomes one with her cloak.

She is so radiant, so lovely that my heart could burst with pride that she's my sister. She gives me a tremulous little wave and she looks so small in the moonlight that I can hardly stop myself from rushing down there right that very moment to stop her from going. She's doing this for me. And something is not right. Something is very wrong.

Mum takes Alice's hand and pulls her away and she's saying, "Don't take any notice of Rosa, she's always been a misery guts."

Thanks, dear supportive mother.

"I was just saying goodbye," says Alice, and she turns once more and her wondrous gaze soars like a bird up into the air and in through the bedroom window to land in my heart. Which is quite poetic really.

I see Megan then. She whizzes up behind Mum and Alice at an unnatural speed, WHOOOOOSH, her feet hardly touching the ground. Then just as she gets level with them she hunches up and walks like an old woman. Unaware, Alice takes one of her hands and one of Mum's and they disappear into the shadows.

That's enough watching and wondering and worrying for me.

I have to get going.

Boots on quickly, the dry one and the still damp

one. Bending over to tie the laces, from my upside down vantage point I can see the mirror. In it, Alice's reflection stares at me, terrified. I straighten up quickly, look in the mirror again. There's no reflection in it at all. Not even mine.

I race from the room.

There's no point in bothering to creep past Dad, still slumped over his drawings at the kitchen table. It would take an atom bomb to rouse him. One that explodes, I mean. Several atom bombs probably.

Outside now, I run. At least, my body performs all the actions, arms pumping, knees bending and straightening, feet kicking out, but I don't seem to be getting anywhere. I shout Alice's name, but no sound comes out of my mouth.

I'm heading for the clearing, the clearing with the altar, that's where I'm heading, but something has other ideas. However hard I struggle to move in one direction for some reason my body goes relentlessly in another.

I scream into the night sky, in a rather over-dramatic way, "Don't make me do this, I have to protect Alice," but no-one is listening and I'm dragged on and on through Wayland Woods until...The Horrible Site appears quite suddenly through the trees.

No more struggling.

I'm there. But not where I thought I wanted to be.

Something makes me stay, just for a minute, just to see.

"Then I'll find Alice," I promise. "Then I'll make sure nothing bad happens to her."

Chapter 87

Dark clouds loom overhead casting an eerie blanket of gloom over the trees. It's broken by gaudy flashes of yellow and orange, the safety jackets, the barrier tape, the painted crosses on vehicles and buildings. No crosses on the trees, ha ha!

There's a solitary lumberjack under a dazzling security light. He pulls the cord on a chain-saw again and again trying to start it. It won't and he throws it down in disgust. Then it leaps into life of its own accord and thrashes a path towards his legs. He shrieks in panic and disappears in the night. Serves him right.

Then I gasp without meaning to.

Bates walks the perimeter barrier tape with his dogs. Funny, but I almost call out to him, thinking, "He'll help me, won't he? He's a kind man at heart."

But what if he doesn't? What if he stops me from going to Alice? I stay silent.

He carries a huge flashlight and all around him there are scuffling sounds. He's jumpy, as jumpy as I am which is very jumpy. He directs the beam of light here and there and indistinct shapes scurry into the darkness.

With horrible certainty I realise what he's up to. He's heading straight for the wire mesh fence that surrounds the pheasant breeding pens, he's undoing the padlock on the gate, he's going to shoot the birds, that's what he's doing, isn't it? I can't bear it and charge out of the undergrowth towards him, pumped up with rage.

Then I stop. And smile. And hide again.

He's not shooting them. He's setting them free. With his huge hands he guides them, one after another, drowsy bundles of feathers out into the night and his daft dogs lollop around getting under his feet, tails wagging.

Now, in the distance, I can hear the sound of chanting, drum beats, the crackle of a fire. The Ritual.

Alice.

I have to get there.

Bates hears it too, mutters to the dogs, "Highfalutin' hippies, eh, boys? Less sense than they were born with."

From perfect stillness, a howling wind erupts, circling the site strong enough to knock the flashlight from Bates' grasp. It hits the ground

BANG

and it extinguishes. The dogs yelp and cringe. Bates scoops them up, one under each arm, and battles towards his land-rover.

The wind whirls and whooshes around the edge of The Horrible Site, round and round like a tornado, deafening me with its roar yet I'm standing a few feet from it and the air is completely still.

These days I'm growing quite accustomed to Nature and the way it has of making itself clear to anyone sensible enough to listen.

Like me.

Chapter 88

Nothing stops me from getting close to Alice this time. I've seen what I was meant to see at The Horrible Site and now it's okay to go.

And there they all are at the altar, lit by moonlight and torches, silver and flickering gold. And part of me wants to laugh again, the part of me that thinks this is all one big idiotic harmless game played by adults who've drunk too much cider or been out in the sun too long. But there's another part of me, a tight little knot of doubt deep inside me, pushing its way towards the surface.

So I don't laugh.

I *almost* laugh though, picking out the Distinguished People of Wayland Village Who Should Know Better clustered in little groups waiting for the ceremony to begin, the men wearing ridiculous antlers on their heads and the women with crowns of flowers.

There's The Vicar, The Station Master with the mad wandering eye, the Very Small Man with the streaky hair who works in the butcher's, Dreadlock Man who cuts the grass in the churchyard...

Then of course, there's Gloria, pacing up and down wringing her hands and there's Megan, all hunched and wizened like an old crow. And there's the masked Green Boy again, no antlers on his head, leaning up against a tree watching everyone like the Incredible Hulk only way more puny. There's no Rhodri to be seen which is just as well for Mum, I suppose, or she'd run gibbering all the way home.

And then there's Alice.

Alice lies on the altar. She wears her pure white dress and a wreath of lilies and she looks horribly *dead,* to be honest, but she isn't because she's fidgeting and sometimes smiling when people talk to her. She's often swamped in a tide of people, who coo over her, touch her hair, her cheeks and Gloria swoops on her like a bird of prey.

At one end of the altar there's a huge jar and the more I look at it the more can I see that it's in the shape of a womb, or uterus if you want to be technical. Gross and double gross. I can tell the shape from a picture there is in my Biology book at school. It's a sort of roundy triangle with curly arm things coming out of either side of the top. Check it out in your own Biology book if you don't believe me.

Then...the drumbeats rise to an unnerving crescendo.

And The Ritual begins.

Chapter 89

I don't know what to call him any more because he's certainly nothing like any vicar I've ever met (which is very few) but The Vicar will have to do. That or The King of The Freaky People. Anyway, everyone gathers round him and he launches into crazy chant mode, booming,

> "Cast the magic spell about,
> to keep the evil spirits out."

...and he draws pentagrams (five-pointed stars, in case you didn't know) in the air at each corner of the altar with vast sweeps of his bony arms. Then he declares, like some sort of Shakespearean actor blokie,

> "To make the spell forever thine,
> let it now be spake in rhyme."

Which doesn't even rhyme, itself. Not really, anyway. Maybe he writes stuff to go inside old people's birthday cards when he takes a break from being a creepy vicar.

The next bit makes me want to puke.

The Vicar seizes the uterus jar by its handles and holds it high above his head then Gloria and The Green Boy, who wears the hugest antlers now, do this weird suggestive dance in the middle of a ring of leering people, all writhing and pouting and pelvic thrusts and general total embarrassing grossness.

Gloria ought to pick someone her own age in my opinion.

And The Vicar shouts to the skies, "Our fires burns stronger, ever stronger, the fires of Lust and Passion. We know that like the earth around us, beneath us, within us, we too are fertile."

And as he shouts and they writhe, the trees around the clearing sprout new growth and begin to close in on everyone inch by inch, inch by creeping inch, and nobody notices but me and Megan, who whirls around, her eyes glinting with delight.

Pushing my way through the spreading foliage round to the end of the altar, I can see the top of Alice's head in front of me through the twisted branches and I'm calling out her name but it's drowned out by the rising frenzy of drums and chants and The Vicar approaches the altar and he clasps a silver dagger, his hands raised above his head and he brings it down between Alice's legs screaming, "Accept our sacrifice! Bring us fertility, we implore you!"

And I'm screaming too as redness spurts upwards in a startling arc.

Then Alice sits up, smiling sweetly, and climbs down from the altar, her white dress splattered with ripe watermelon flesh. The fruit itself lies split in two, oozing vermilion stickiness in the light of the fire.

And everyone claps and cheers.

And I feel like a total numpty.

And The Green Boy is pushed towards Gloria by the leering people and he's prodded and poked until he mumbles, "I am the mighty oak tree, the pride of the forest. I am the rutting stag. I am the giver of seed, the power of life."

But he's not any of those things.

I recognise his voice.

It's Kieron.

I don't have time to feel any of the feelings that splurge into my mind at that precise moment.

Which is probably just as well.

Megan circles, cackling with glee. Alice carries a bowl containing white powder to the fire. Her sweet voice rises above the rest of the noise.

"I am the child of violet fire...
My virginal purity,
Is earth's sole desire!"

She throws the powder into the flames. There's an ear-splitting crack, a blinding flash of violet...

And Alice disappears.

And so does Megan.

Chapter 90

I break through into the clearing amidst a smattering of applause from the Freaky People who stumble around bumping into each other, still half-blinded by the flash and stunned by the noise. The applause isn't for me. They haven't seen me. While I'm tearing around looking for Alice, they're busy applauding The Vicar.

"How did you do that?" asks The Very Small Man.

"That was far out, Vicar. Awesome!" says Dreadlock Man.

"But where's Alice?" says a small voice that is Mum's. Perhaps my mother has finally come to her senses? It's only taken her thirty seven years.

"Ah, Alice. That's Megan's department," says The Vicar modestly. "If you must know, she arranged the whole thing."

Mum says, "But where's Megan? I can't see Megan either."

The Vicar smiles and says, "She's taking Alice home to sleep at her house so we can…" then he gives a salacious wink, "carry on. Gloria's ready for it now, aren't you Gloria?"

"Oh, fine," says Mum suffused with relief, "But I wonder why Megan didn't tell me?"

And I despair of all adults everywhere.

At that moment, I see Alice. Her face is whiter than her dress. She's being drawn backwards into the clutches of the trees, branch by grasping branch. A large hare leaps after her. And so do I, right past a startled Kieron.

The undergrowth parts to let me through then closes behind me. I glance back and Kieron has ripped off his mask and then he's out of my sight, obscured by the branches.

The last voice I hear from the clearing is Gloria's.
"My rutting stag has fled," she says disconsolately.

Chapter 91

On and on I go after Alice. Hand-like branches claw at her, pass her backwards from tree to tree. She cries out, her arms outstretched towards me calling out, "Rosa, Rosa, help me!"

Ahead, the hare runs, glancing back every so often. I duck under low branches, beat them aside with dogged determination, desperate to save Alice. Once, just once, I manage to reach her, touch her fingertips, but she's whipped away again.

Dawn streaks the sky. Closer and closer we get to The Horrible Site and the wind still howls around the boundaries, a thunderous, booming hurricane. The woods are less dense now and ahead of me, ahead of poor frightened Alice, I can see building site materials flying through the air, tarpaulins, sacks, fluorescent jackets, signs, all whirling dangerously, and there is Bates' Land Rover, buffeted by the force of the wind, wheels spinning desperately in a ditch as he tries to make his escape.

Then Alice is whisked upwards out of the trees like a piece of tissue, flailing her arms wildly and I think "That's it. She's done for. I'll never see her again." But somehow, the hurricane is above me and I blunder onwards trying to keep her in my sight.

Behind me someone shouts, "Rosa, Rosa," and I think it must be Bates but the voice is snatched away by the fierce clutches of the wind.

We're right in the middle of the site now, me struggling to pick a path through the devastation, the hare still bounding ahead of me, Alice carried along like she's above me and then unexpectedly just when I can't go on any longer, the wind drops and Alice is deposited quite gently in a crumpled heap in front of me, beneath a gnarled old oak tree. And the hare disappears into a gaping hole at its base.

I run to her, to my little sister. "Oh Alice," I say. "Oh Alice!" And I take her in my arms, feeling quite gooey with unexpected emotion.

"I did it for you," she says. "Can you feel your face getting better yet?"

"Oh Alice," I say again. The goo must be affecting my brain.

Alice begins to cry. "But Megan said..." she sobs and I hold her close. Then I clamber slowly to my feet and pull Alice to hers.

And HISSSSSSSSSSSSS!

Megan darts out from the depths of the tree, pounces on Alice and forces her towards the hole in the tangled roots.

"No! Let her go!" I yell, and dive towards her but Megan holds me back with a strength I'd have thought impossible for such a small old woman if I hadn't felt her bony fingers digging into my arm.

"Mother Earth desires her, her purity," Megan hisses. She's as crazy as a soup sandwich. I can cope with crazy but...wicked supernatural powers? I'm not so sure.

She gestures with her other wizened hand at the site, trampled by men's heavy boots, carved up by machine tracks, prepared for utter destruction. "Mother Earth must be appeased for all *this*."

"Yes, but not this way," I blurt.

Ghostly green hands snake out of the tree, caress Alice's face, paw at her, throttle her. In the air, or in my head, there's a moaning and a whispering in Megan's distorted voice, "Alice, Alice, Alice has the purity Mother Earth desires."

"I'll do it," I shout. Anything to shut the voice up. "I'll stop the destruction of Wayland Woods. Just don't harm Alice."

"You?" sneers Megan, "You? How? You are incapable."

Her face warps and cracks into a hideously contorted mass of bone and gristle, then mutates to a bleached hare skull, bulbous jelly eyes still protruding from sockets. I watch, like you can't help watching a car crash, mesmerised, disgusted and terrified all in the same moment.

"You?" The word spits from between her mangled lips on a fetid spurt of foul breath.

I want to turn away before I'm liquefied in the vileness but there's Alice. It's for Alice. For Alice I don't turn away though vomit rises in my throat and threatens to spew.

"Just let her go and take me, if that's what you want," says my voice, not belonging to me at all.

"You? Why would anyone want you?"

Why would anyone want me? The thought's always been there.

"Because I care."

Did I really say that? I'm not sure.

But the moaning stops and the ghostly ghastly green hands round Alice's neck slither away. And Megan's not there anymore, thank goodness, but the hare's back again.

And with a flick of its bobtail it vanishes once more into the tree.

The wind circles the site one last time whispering, "She will show us how, she will show us or Alice is surely lost."

Things like this never happen in Notting Hill.

Chapter 92

Now what am I supposed to do?

How about pretend it never happened? That's what grown ups do, isn't it? (Well, all the grown-ups I know). Maybe it's a sign of maturity?

Alice is shivering so much I lend her my sweatshirt in a noble gesture of self-sacrifice but now I'm shivering too. Self-sacrifice is over-rated.

Then the sun breaks through the mist that shrouds the trees around the site and it's breath-taking in its beauty.

Dream-catching fairy story magical.

Alice and I just gaze and gaze and drink it all in greedily as though we're parched from too much ugliness in the world and we wait for our blood to be warmed so we have enough energy to move.

We have to move. The Horrible Site is coming to life too, harsh and jagged against the soft folds of the trees, vehicles moving, men arriving, cursing at the havoc played by last night's wind.

"They are making a bit of a mess of Wayland Woods, aren't they?" says Alice, in the perfect simple way she has of always getting right to the heart of things.

"I know they are," I answer, "And it's partly Dad's fault too. I can't bear it. Let's go home."

"But you *promised*," says Alice, in the perfect simple way she has of always getting right to the heart of things. Again.

But this is something I don't want to hear.

"Before I do anything else, I'm getting you home," I say firmly.

She doesn't argue. I'm hoping she can't read my mind because once we're there, my plan is to crawl up the stairs to my lumpy little bed and go to sleep.

At once, a sharp breeze spirals through the trees making the leaves rustle resentfully.

I ignore it.

Yes I know. I have about as much integrity as a cockroach, but I'm very, very tired. Indeed.

And have I ever mentioned that Alice can be very annoying sometimes?

Chapter 93

Arm in arm we wander along the path between the trees, not talking much because we're both exhausted and I'm busily persuading myself that I'm doing the right thing and all that stuff about Alice being dragged through the trees and surely lost forever was A Figment Of My Imagination.

I'm getting quite good at this selective believing thing. I suppose it's a bit like religion.

Then we come across Kieron fast asleep under a tree like a giant mottled green slug. Boy, does he look a sight and it isn't until I kick him (not very hard) in the ribs and he wakes up with a start that I remember that I must look a sight too and wish I'd just left him being a slug.

The first thing he says is, "I couldn't find you. I was pretty worried." And my heart does a little lurch until I work out that he must mean Alice.

But his green eyes are on me and it's a feeling that I'm not used to. Not the feeling that I'm being stared at because that's something I'm very used to , believe me, but the feeling that I'm being stared at and it doesn't make me want to shrivel up and die.

"Rosa kept hugging her boot for hours after you brought it back," says Alice and then I probably do want to shrivel up and die.

But Kieron smiles and it is a real smile and we walk along together, the three of us, and it's nice except I'm not sure about Alice being here but it's probably a good thing in the circumstances, rather like having a dog.

"Rutting stag, eh?" I say.

He smiles again. "My guilty secret. I told Caitlin I'd cut her tongue out with a pair of blunt scissors if she ever let on to you."

And I want to ask him why on earth does he do something so demeaning? But before I open my mouth he tells me, which is another weird feeling that I've only ever had with Alice before but she's a relative.

"It's so I can keep an eye on my dad."

"And then he didn't even turn up," he finishes.

I wonder if I should tell him about that, but we're just crossing one of the wide tracks that leads to The Horrible Site when things suddenly go into freefall again.

Chapter 94

Bouncing and bumping along the track comes a very sleek, shiny four-wheel-drive vehicle with not a speck of dirt on it, like you might see on the Kings Road in Chelsea stuffed with bratty kids being taken three yards down the road to their posh private school.

At the wheel is Tristan. It's easy to tell it's him by the pink blubbery face grinning through the windscreen as he almost mows us down. He shudders to a halt (the 4x4 does, at least) and we all walk a bit faster to get away from him but he jumps out in front of us with a riding crop in his hand and no horse.

"Well, well, well, what a bedraggled little bunch of miscreants we have here," he says, oddly ignoring the fact that two of us were guests at his house only the other day and that Alice has just been horribly sacrificed on an altar all in an effort to sort out Gloria's womb malfunctions.

"New every morning is the love," says Alice obscurely, by way of greeting, and then she curtseys. Why did she have to go and do that?

Tristan regards her as he might do a piece of dog shit stuck to his shoe and I regard him like an even bigger piece of dog shit brought indoors on a shoe and smeared onto the living room carpet. Kieron's fists clench but that's all, as far as I can tell. Long years of practice at being a peasant, I expect.

"I'd offer you a lift only I've just had my car professionally valeted," says Tristan "I was thinking you might want to come and watch the fun."

"Fun?"

"You know," he says, "The End of Wayland Woods As We Know It." And he swishes his riding crop viciously again and again in the air inches from

Kieron's nose yelling

"TIMMMMBERRRRRR."

Kieron doesn't even blink.

"Oh, Wilding," he scoffs at him as he gets into his stupid pretentious vehicle again, "Did I mention the eviction order? No? Ooooh, slap wrist time, it must have slipped my mind. Your... bijou residence stands in the way of progress."

Then he starts the engine and rockets off towards the site, leaving a choking cloud of diesel exhaust in his wake.

"I have to get home, Rosa," Kieron says.

"Is Tristan one of those bloody bastards Caitlin talks about?" asks Alice, and even that isn't enough to make me smile.

"Take Alice," I say to Kieron. More of a command really.

"What?" he asks.

"Please take Alice and look after her for me."

"Where are you going?"

"Back," I say, and turn to go before I change my mind.

Chapter 95

In the air there's the threatening rumble of heavy machinery and the shrill whine of chainsaws. Not far away I can see a line of yellow bulldozers grinding and trundling along the track towards the centre of Wayland Woods.

It isn't wide enough for those ravening monsters but they crunch onwards, crashing through trees and bushes, which splinter in their path like lollipop sticks in a shredder. I think I can hear the screams of agony as each one falls but that's just madness, isn't it?

From somewhere, my exhausted legs find a spurt of energy and I sprint across the uneven ground towards them, past them.

Between them and the site.

On the lead bulldozer, Tristan rides shotgun, his face ablaze with excitement. I can hear him shouting "Yee Hah" as he whips the side of the cab with his riding crop. He's such a pillock. But pillocks are usually harmless, as idiots go, and what he's responsible for is anything but.

I don't know what to do.

So I do the only thing I can think of doing without thinking very much, which is to stand in the middle of the track, my back to the site and my arms stretched out sideways blocking their path. How ridiculous and pathetic is that?

So I stand there and think of that James Bond film where the skier is sucked up in the snow plough and the snow squirts out blood red with his mangled body.

And the bulldozer gets closer and I wonder if the driver has seen me.

And I think of that student in Tienanmen Square in front of the tank and then decide I must be having delusions of grandeur.

And the bulldozer gets closer and the driver *has* seen me and his face is fixed, determined, and he accelerates.

And I think of my life flashing before my eyes which it does when you're about to die and wonder how long it will take. Not many seconds when you're only fourteen, I expect.

And the bulldozer gets closer. And Tristan leans out of the cab window and yells, "Hug a bloody tree somewhere else, shit-for-brains," which isn't very aristocratic of him.

And the blade of the bulldozer towers above me glinting fiercely and still I stand there like an idiot with my arms stretched out.

And behind me on the site, there's a new, deeper thundering sound and underneath me the ground shudders and Tristan screams and there's a hissing of air brakes and a grinding of metal against metal and the bulldozer's only six inches from me and I can taste its diesel-breath in my mouth.

And then it stops.

And I turn, and as I do, huge cracks open up in the ground and there are men running in every direction, flinging chainsaws from their hands and the site huts and the vehicles marked with orange crosses, and all the equipment and materials pitch and roll as though they're on a stormy sea. The clearing breaks apart with a final heaving fracture and the whole lot is swallowed up into the earth.

And through the trees there comes a whispering, "She has shown us, she has shown us…"

And it's as if The Horrible Site was never there except for a single strip of black and yellow barrier tape flapping on a branch.

Chapter 96

I did it!
I
Me
Rosa Cavanagh
All on my own
Did
It
I think.

Chapter 97

There's still the plume of smoke wafting skywards in the hot summer sun when I approach the Wilding's cottage but, I don't know quite how to explain it, there's an air about the place that's different, somehow.

I haven't time to work out what it is. I'm dying to see Alice. Oh, and Kieron. I almost forgot to mention him. And that's a joke, by the way. I'd put Kieron first, actually. It seems safe now to admit that.

He's waiting outside for me and he's washed off the green paint mostly and I want to run into his arms in slow motion like Cathy and Heathcliff in *Wuthering Heights* but that wouldn't be particularly cool so I stride up to him instead and say, "You scrub up well for a peasant," and he thumps me on the arm.

Then it all comes pouring out of me in a torrent of words, everything that's happened and that it doesn't look as though the cottage is under threat anymore and he says, "Well, come inside and tell everyone."

That makes me hesitate and he knows what's on my mind without me having to speak again, which is very comforting. He says, "Don't worry, Dad's not in," and takes me by the hand so I almost melt and we go into the kitchen.

The kitchen is clean, sparkling clean and tidy and there's a flame-haired woman there polishing spoons until they shine. She looks like Caitlin much older and there's Caitlin too who flings herself at me wreathed in smiles and says, "She's back! She's come back!" and the woman says, "Who's she? The cat's mother?" and hugs Caitlin so it's just like a proper family. Unlike mine.

Alice. I suddenly remember Alice and there she is curled up fast asleep in a rocking chair wrapped in a patchwork quilt.

"Bless her, she was all done in, poor lambkin," says Caitlin's mum and I can't help thinking two things:

1. Caitlin's mum doesn't seem very much like a slag. Not that I know very much about them, to be honest, but surely they aren't meant be like that, all homely and smelling of apples.
2. I wish she was my mum.
3. I suppose at least my mum didn't run off and leave me and Alice with a drunken father. Oh, that's three things.

Then...

The door flies open and there's Rhodri all dishevelled and grizzly and miserable and probably about to swear at me until he notices the state of the kitchen and then he notices Caitlin's mum standing there, leaning against the sink, her arms folded and she says, "What sort of time do you call this?"

Chapter 98

It's quite late in the morning by the time I get Alice home but it doesn't matter because Mum and Dad are still in bed. Other times I'd think, "Oh, what concerned and responsible parents they are, not, " but today it's just a relief that there's no explaining to do.

Two things happen later in the day – well, lots of things happen, of course, like we have a very late breakfast and I don't bother to make my bed - but two things in particular.

And one thing makes me laugh and the other thing makes me cry even though my heart is so full of Kieron that crying doesn't come that easily.

The laughing bit.

Dad's in the kitchen slouching over his tenth cup of fierce black coffee and nursing The Worst Hangover in the History of All Hangovers Ever, when Tristan comes bursting in through the door which is rather a shock to everyone, especially Tristan who has probably never been in such a small, low-ceilinged room.

For a moment I think he's come to complain about me and my death-defying act of madness but he hasn't at all. In fact, he doesn't even register I'm in the kitchen, as far as I know.

He bounds over to Dad and gives him a jovial slap on the back which makes Dad groan quite badly, and Alice giggle, then he says, "Kevin old man, forget the golf complex. Crazy scheme. Don't know what we were thinking."

Dad unfolds himself into an upright position then immediately regrets it, clutches his head and mumbles, "What are you talking about, Tristan?"

"Biospheres! That's what I'm talking about. A stroke of genius. How about it?"

A little spark of enthusiasm ignites in Dad's eyes and begins to flicker dimly. "Biospheres!" he murmurs...

"I reckon that earth tremor actually did us a huge favour," Tristan goes on.

"Earth tremor?" says Dad. "What are you talking about?" Yes, what is he talking about? Doesn't he know that it was Mother Nature wreaking her revenge?

"Oh, and another thing," says Tristan, completely ignoring Dad's question. "Seems Gloria's expecting. Has been for weeks, apparently."

"What is she expecting?" asks Alice. "The unexpected?"

Tristan looks at Alice as though he is wondering if fatherhood is such a good idea after all.

Chapter 99

The crying bit.

Mum's nowhere to be seen after lunch and come to think of it, she's hardly said a word since Tristan left. Not that she had much opportunity with Dad burbling on about the biospheres at the Eden Project, when he hasn't even been there and I have.

An itsy-bitsy thought flits into my brain that she may have run off because of Dad's drinking. That's until I remember it was Mum who got him drunk.

Still, where *is* she?

She's shut herself in the bedroom, that's where. All on her own and her eyes are red and swollen and in one hand she holds that photo of her and Deborah and keeps stroking it as though it's the most precious thing in the world to her.

"Mum?"

I perch on the end of her bed and she doesn't even look up.

"Mum, won't you come to the churchyard with me?"

She shakes her head so hard that bits of leaf and fluff fly off in all directions which would have been amusing in different circumstances.

"I can't, Rosa. Don't you see? I can't."

"You could if I came with you."

As soon as the words spurt out of my mouth I wish they hadn't. Mainly because sometimes it's easier being an ostrich with your head stuck in the sand so you don't have to face up to things that are difficult, despite getting a load of grit in your eyes. Also because I'm not sure which version of reality there might be in the churchyard when we get there.

"Would you come?" asks Mum, her eyes big round

surprises.

"Of course!" - said with more confidence than I'm feeling just at the moment.

So we go, and we take flowers from the garden and it's the first time we've gone anywhere together for about a hundred years. And I don't have to hint and prod or anything like that because the story of her and Rhodri and Deborah comes out in a trickle that grows into a torrent. And she's so busy remembering that she doesn't notice Megan, carrying a battered old suitcase, getting on to the bus in the village square. But I do.

"You see," says Mum, "In those days, there wasn't the make-up like you use, Rosa. People wouldn't even know you had a birthmark, but for her it was different."

My teeth are clamped over my tongue to stop me from disagreeing with her because, up until today, my life has completely sucked. At school in Notting Hill, people called me Blaze of Gory. (No I don't mean Glory). Not to my face, but somehow that almost made it worse.

"She adored him, completely adored him, and he couldn't even bear to look at her."

Inside I bled for her. Outside, Mum wept, but I don't know who for.

"And then one day, Deborah and I fell out. I can't even remember what it was about. Something silly, I expect. Like you and Alice fall out over silly things."

Tongue-clamping time again.

"And to spite her, I…" Mum stops walking towards the churchyard and her whole frame kind of shudders.

"You what?"

Mum's voice gets so quiet it's hard to pick out the words. "I went after Rhodri even though I didn't like him very much."

My turn to stop walking, wanting to run, put distance between us, but Mum grabs my arm and says

"Please, Rosa!" in such a piteous voice that I stay but my face must give away the sickening disgust.

She carries on with the self-annihilation and it's one of those occasions where you don't want to hear and you do want to hear at the same time like passing a horrendous pile-up on a motorway and you just have to look.

"And we were outside Rhodri's cottage and she was watching from the trees and…" Without realising, I put my hands over my ears but I still hear it.

"…and I saw her and laughed and kissed Rhodri full on the lips. And that's when she…"

Then I do run.

Into the churchyard.

And Deborah's grave is there in the corner and I fling myself to the ground beside it and sob until I run out of sobs and there are sobs carrying on even when mine have stopped and those belong to Mum.

She kneels down beside me and takes me in her arms, and my legs that want to kick her and fists that want to punch her change their minds.

"Can you ever forgive me?" she says, over and over again and I don't know if she's talking to me or Deborah.

"Yes, I can," I answer and don't know if I'm speaking for myself.

Then all the sobbing stops.

Chapter 100

The river's become a special place now. I feel as though I belong there.

Kieron and I spend most of our time here and it's a little piece of heaven, even when Caitlin and Alice want to come too, which they did today.

Kieron and I sit with our backs against a tree and wherever our bodies touch I can feel the warmth of his and there's not a better feeling in the world than our closeness and I can't imagine that there ever will be.

Caitlin lies stretched out full length at our feet, making buttercup and daisy chains into a crown for me, the Queen of Lurve as she calls me, until I hit her or Kieron does.

Alice dozes, head in my lap. She murmurs, "S'funny, Rosa."

"What's funny, Alice? Apart from you."

"Well there's no Megan anymore, is there?"

Caitlin and I exchange glances. Hers is more venomous than mine.

"Maybe that's for the best, Alice," I say, because I'm diplomatic.

"She's just weird and I hope her brain rots and her toes drop off," said Caitlin, because she's not.

Alice doesn't notice. She says, "And my beautiful hare suit…"

"What about it?"

"I couldn't find it anywhere and then I did find it and it was all shrivelled up as small as my little finger."

"Really?" Now that *was* quite unexpected.

"So now it doesn't fit me anymore," she went on.

Shame. Not.

Alice hasn't finished.

"S'funny it all came true. The story. I knew it

would."

"What story is this?" asks Kieron and Alice sits up and I only cringe a tiny bit because I know she's going to tell it but don't mind too much. I'd like to hear the end even if it was only something Megan made up.

And this is the end of the story which came true.

Many centuries hence will come a first-born girl. So brave she will be that she may look into the eyes of a man and no damage will befall her and he will turn no more away. She and she alone may end the curse forever.

And the girl-child's name will be Rosa. Blessed will she be.

And Kieron reaches out and feather-light he touches my face.

I don't bother with the make-up these days. The birthmark is much paler now.

"Does it hurt?" he asks.

"Not any more," I reply.

(blurb)

When Rosa's uprooted from civilised Notting Hill to her mum's ramshackle family home in deepest Somerset, she's furious.

Strange druidic rituals, an unexplained death, and airy-fairy sister Alice's life in peril at the hands of a malevolent old hag are enough to draw Rosa in to rural life, however hard she fights against it.

And then there's the boy…